THE HIDDEN GRAVEYARD

THE WHISPER INVESTIGATIONS TRILOGY

MARC LAYTON

I

1

Sirens blared, and through blurred vision, a string of red and blue lights began to appear through a tree line. Hours passed by. Three? Ten? I didn't know anymore. Numbness crept through my body, confusion clouding my mind and strangling my lungs. Despair felt like a place I would never leave. So, I ran.

I ran into the trees, branches slapping my face as I plunged deeper and deeper into the woods. Tripping on a rough, twisted branch, I fell face first down a muddy, rocky hill. The cold morning breeze beat against my pale, thin skin until I landed at the bottom of the endless pit. I curled into a ball, finally able to feel pain, legs pulled up into my chest, and began to weep. The sound echoed in the silence around me as my sobs grew louder.

Utterly alone, I tried to breathe deeply into my lungs, but I couldn't. It felt like someone was holding their hand over my mouth, like they were trying to suffocate me, pulling me into the earth. I didn't know what this force was or where it came from. I gave in, feeling the darkness overtake me and push me further into the ground.

2

My eyes shot open as I gasped for air. Reality sank in quickly. Regaining my composure, I shuffled into the living room of my apartment to find my older brother passed out on the couch.

I switched on the coffee pot and began to brew each of us a cup. He was probably still drunk. He awoke with a jump as I set his mug down on the glass coffee table a little louder than necessary.

He glared at me. "What's got you up so early?"

"It's 11 AM...on a Sunday. You should probably get up. You didn't want to sleep in the spare?"

He snatched the coffee cup and sat up. "No. I did not want to sleep in that bright green room. Besides, I came in late."

I rolled my eyes as we each sipped our coffee, checking news updates and social media feeds. Eventually, he got up and walked silently over to the sink to clean his mug. This was when I knew something was wrong.

Wary of him, I asked, "Damian, what's wrong?"

"Huh? Nothing's wrong. What's wrong with you?"

"You never clean your mugs when you're hungover. You always sleep in that bright green room you don't like, and I've known you your entire life - you've never gone this long without saying something."

He looked down at the countertop with his arms spread, palms flat out on the surface. Taking a deep breath, he put his head in his hands, propping himself up with his elbows.

"Liam..."

"No," I interrupted, "We are not doing this. We're not having this conversation again."

Damian looked at me again with raised eyebrows. He seemed to stare straight into my soul. Every time Damian wanted to do something, we both knew we would end up doing it, no matter how much I protested. But this was the only thing I had kept pushing back. Maybe it was finally time to give in. I was just so worried.

He had large brown eyes like mine, except his were darker. We looked so much alike that strangers always thought we were twins. As we grew older, it became easier to tell us apart. My hair turned a dusty blonde, and I always kept it short. His became dark hazelnut, and he kept it on the longer side, although never past his shoulders.

We were both tall, around six feet, and generally handsome, though I didn't focus on women at all. Damian was always the flirt. I just laughed and pretended not to notice women. They caused more trouble for me.

I liked my day routine and organized, and adding a woman into the mix was too chaotic. I had been diagnosed with OCD as a child, but I didn't think much of it. The only thing I enjoyed was having a routine, and I didn't see anything wrong with that.

"Damian, I'm serious. This could be dangerous. We don't know what's out there. We're not detectives!"

"Liam...I got fired."

Staring at him in shock, I asked, "When?!"

"Last night."

"I'm so sorry. I had no idea. Is that why you want to go now? Because you feel like you can?"

He sighed and thought it over. "I guess. I've been bouncing around jobs my entire life. It feels like it's looming in the back of my mind, all the time. I can't focus. I can't get anything done."

Our parents' death had always been hard on him. He didn't know what to do with himself half the time—trying to raise me and constantly worrying about if he was doing the right thing.

We'd never found out what happened to our parents. Early one morning on one of our camping trips, they went into the woods, and just like that, vanished into thin air.

The police never found them, even after they interrogated everyone around the camp. No one had seen anything, and no witnesses had ever come forward. It had been, and still was, frustrating, to say the least. Damian was twelve at the time, and I was eight. Neither one of us understood, but Damian seemed to change immediately. He became my protector, the one who took care of me. The one who made sure the relatives we bounced around between were giving me the best life I could have.

"You still dream about them, don't you?"

I reluctantly sighed and nodded my head.

"They're out there. Their bodies are out there, somewhere. They couldn't have just disappeared into nothingness. I have this feeling..." he paused, contemplating his words carefully, "...that maybe, they could still be here. In spirit, watching us. Waiting for us to find them."

"You think they are haunting you?"

Damian had always had some strange ideas, but this one was a bit too out there. I worked in an office, and I had things to do, a life to live. He wanted me to drop it all so he could follow the wishes of our parents, find their bodies. It sounded insane to me.

"It's serious stuff! I saw a documentary. I know they're waiting for us to figure out what happened that night. It's like they're on one side of the glass screaming at me, and I'm on the other trying to hear, but nothing is coming in clearly."

The more I thought about it, the more I talked myself into finally letting him live his dream. He wanted this more than anything. He has asked me at least once per year since our late teens. He'd always protected me as the older brother, so why couldn't I let him have this one thing? I couldn't say no.

I scoffed, not wanting to seem to give in too easily. "Okay, whatever you say."

"So you're in?! Great. I already brought my bag."

He pulled out a large blue backpack filled to the brim with his belongings. I sulked to my room and began packing my identical bag in red. They were well-made and large, usually used for long-distance hikers, but we used them because we moved around so often. We could fit our lives into these small packs. Thankfully, as men in our 30s, we didn't need to live that way anymore.

He had already packed his truck with our tent and fire supplies. It was then that I realized he had planned on going alone if I hadn't agreed. Stubborn. The trip was long, about two hours until we would arrive in Sonora Park. It was a tiny town, but the park and camping grounds were usually fully booked all summer. Lucky for us, Damian had already thought of that too and secured us a spot.

3

As we approached the town, we saw a small bar on the side of the road. The sign read *Bailee's*, and there were at least five motorcycles outside waiting for their owners.

Run-down didn't even begin to describe the place. Compared to our larger suburb, this place was a dump. Unfortunately, it was our only option to get a quick bite before setting up for the night. We entered and were seated at a booth by an older woman who knew everyone's names but ours.

In a matter of minutes, we had burgers and fries in front of us. For a small shabby place, the service was excellent. Damian and I tried to eat quickly and not talk much; we knew we only had so long before dark. We were anxious to get to the park and get settled for the night. After a few minutes into our meal, a middle-aged man strolled up to our table.

"Are you guys from around here? I haven't seen you here before."

Damian raised his eyebrows slightly towards me as if to say, *Is this guy joking?*

"I asked you a question." The man began to speak more aggressively when we didn't answer right away. "We don't want any trouble. We're going to the campgrounds not too far from here."

He glanced back at his buddies. "Oh? The campgrounds. How cute! Maybe you can pick us some berries while you're there."

I could see the anger start to rise in Damian. He didn't tolerate toxic men who felt the need to constantly bring people down. He locked eyes with me, trying to remain as calm as he could - which wasn't very calm at all.

The man continued despite our efforts to ignore him. "Little boys going back to mom and dad at the park?"

As the man inched toward him, I saw the far-away look in Damian's eyes, and his hands slowly turned to fists. He couldn't resist any longer. He raised his fist in an uppercut motion, swinging through the hefty man's chin. The man's friends stood still, silently shocked by the guts of the guy who had just started a fight with the biggest man in the bar. The large man stood and grappled at Damian's legs, dragging him to the ground.

They began to wrestle, everyone staring, unsure of what to do or how to stop it - until one small woman came forward and pushed the man off of Damian. She stood just over five feet tall with a slender but toned figure. Her brown, flat bangs swung across her forehead, the rest of her flowing hair kept behind in a high pony. It wasn't until she helped a drooling Damian off the floor that we both realized she was in uniform.

"I guess that's one way to introduce yourself to the town," she explained as she shot a glare to the big man.

The man gave a quick nod and walked back to his friends without another word. I couldn't tell if he was ashamed that he'd gotten pushed over by a woman or if she had control over this town, but I was just glad he was walking away.

"Meredith Crosby," she extended her hand, "local sheriff's deputy. What's going on today?"

We each shook her hand, and I looked to Damian to speak, but he was tongue-tied by her beauty. An uncomfortably long pause passed before Damian finally spoke up.

"The campground...We're going to the campground down the road."

"Great," she seemed a little taken aback by his demeanor, but not enough that it shook her confidence. "I can give you an escort up there if you'd like?"

Damian nodded in agreement. He stared at the floor in embarrassment. I had never seen him uncomfortable in front of a woman before. He was always confident and even cocky sometimes. It was evident that he was taken aback by this beautiful woman.

She lowered her voice to almost a whisper, "Don't worry about the big guy. He's an idiot. Not the first fight of his I've broken up this week."

As she stepped back, she winked at Damian. He smiled, looking a little dazed.

"Shall we go then?"

We all stepped out to our trucks, Meredith turning on her lights to guide the way. I looked at Damian, who now had his head against the steering wheel in shame. I tried to speak several times, but I wasn't sure what to say.

"Shut up." He lifted his head from the wheel and began to drive away in silent frustration.

As we arrived at the park, Meredith waved to us at the entrance, and we drove to our registered spot. It took longer than expected to set up the tent because we hadn't done this in ages. As the sun began to settle on the horizon, we started our fire and cooked up some brats. We hadn't finished our meal at the bar, so this would have to do.

It was difficult to sleep in the tent, and it didn't help that we were both anxious. It was eerie to be back in the place that had been giving me nightmares for the past 20 years. The last time we were in this campground, in a tent, our parents disappeared forever.

I stared at the blue vinyl siding and pictured our last moments together as a family. Our father telling us goodnight, our mother kissing us on the cheek.

Damian could've been thinking the same thing as he lay awake next to me, but he was more likely replaying the moment he'd had with his newfound love interest from earlier today.

As the sun rose, I'd maybe had a few hours of sleep. Nevertheless, we had work to do. It was time to figure out a few things, and I had no idea where to start.

4

I climbed out of the tent to find Damian with a full breakfast prepared. Eggs, bacon, and toast. We sat and ate, talking through our plan for the day. Neither one of us knew what we were doing.

"What's the plan?"

Damian looked at me, wide-eyed. "You don't have a plan? You always have a plan."

My eyes grew in disbelief. "*You* brought *me* down here, and you don't know what the plan is?"

"Nope."

I took a deep breath to calm myself, taking another bite of my scrambled eggs. We'd both seen thousands of detective shows - what would they do?

"I guess we start in the woods? See if there's anything in there? Maybe there'll be hikers who walk through often. Any ghosts you can see, since you're the ghost whisperer now."

He mocked me and rolled his eyes. "Ghost whisperer. Please."

We finished breakfast and headed out into the woods. The path to the river was short as our site was the closest to it. We began to walk alongside the river, upstream towards an incline. It seemed like the water dove off the side of a cliff, but upon further inspection, we realized the incline was just a hill of more trees and riverside. By midday, we had walked for miles, only stopping for a quick sandwich break.

Far ahead, we spotted an opening in the tree line. A seemingly empty area of the thick woods, but as we approached, we saw a house. Some kind of cabin, maybe a summer home.

I had never seen this cabin before, even though we'd traveled through these woods many times during our childhood. I looked over to Damian to catch him making the same face I was. Confused, yet intrigued. It was definitely old enough that we would have stumbled across it as kids. After searching the yard, we walked up to the large wooden double doors in the front of the home.

Strangely, the home looked well-kept. The front porch didn't creak, the windows looked freshly washed, and the large bulbs in the Victorian-style patio lights were still on and working. It was in good condition. But the yard was a jungle of neglected vines and dead flower beds. It blended in with the forest well, but the home was an immaculate Victorian-style two-story cabin—a vacation home for wealthy folks, perhaps.

I knocked on the door slowly, awaiting a response from some elderly gentleman, like in the movies. Hearing footsteps, I took a step back to join Damian side by side on the porch. The door creaked open to reveal a slim, middle-aged woman in a mid-length yellow dress.

"Can I help you?" she asked politely, confused by our presence.

I couldn't speak. Damian stared at me for a moment and then stepped forward to introduce us both.

"Hi there. I'm Damian, and this is my brother, Liam. We were looking around the area for anyone who might have been here in the summer of 1998. Do you know anyone who might have been here then?"

She looked us both up and down slowly. She stayed silent, evaluating us. Damian glanced at me again and shrugged. We were all staring, until suddenly a taller man appeared from behind her.

"Hey, hey! What's the hold up here?"

She jumped slightly as she turned to meet him. "These men are asking about 1998. Were we up here that summer?"

"Why I'm not sure. Hm...we had to have been because, well... who knows, really?! I'm sure we were, but I can't say for certain. Why don't you boys come in, and you can ask us whatever you need."

Without hesitation, Damian strode into the home of a stranger while I reluctantly followed behind, taking one last look behind us as we ventured inside. The interior wasn't much of a surprise. The well-kept exterior was telling of the interior Victorian-style decor. There was a grand staircase to the right of the front door with sitting rooms on each side.

The man looked well put together. He was clad in business attire with a brown mustache on his thin lips, dripping with elegance. His wife looked meek and untrusting. Her long and straight black hair elongated her thin figure, and her brown eyes were large but sunken into her tan skin. Her lips were plump and covered most of the bottom half of her face as her nose was relatively small.

The woman led us into the kitchen, where the three of us sat at a table and watched her grab a white clay water pitcher and a few glasses. As she filled it up, the man never took his eyes off of us. He wasn't looking at us with any kind of friendliness, but if I had strangers in my home, I guess I would be wary too.

"What did you say your name was?" I asked politely with my hand jutted out to shake his.

He gave me a firm handshake. "Ah! Benjamin. You can call me Ben. And you are?"

"I'm Liam, and this is my brother Damian." I motioned toward him, and he reached out his hand to meet Ben's.

"What's this about you wanting to know about 1998?"

I could tell Damian was about to give away our whole story, but I wasn't going to let him give it up that easy. There was something a little off here in the way the woman wouldn't meet our eyes.

"We grew up not too far from this area and ended up camping at that campground just through the woods. 1998 was the last year we were up here, and we've been looking for some friends of ours that used to camp with us.

"Oh yeah? Well, we've lived here an awfully long time. If you could tell me who you're looking for, maybe I know them!"

He smiled at his wife, who smiled back while carrying the pitcher and cups to the table. She sat beside him, allowing him to continue leading the conversation.

"We're looking for the Sullivans - Nancy and Derrick? They were here around then. Ever heard of them?" Damian chimed in before I could speak.

He pet his mustache. "I don't believe I have."

"You mean the couple who died? Those parents?" The wife blurted out.

Ben looked at her with a mixture of confusion and maybe even frustration. At his gaze, she shrank into her chair as if to let him know she was sorry and she wouldn't speak out of turn again.

"They died? What do you know about that?" I tried to seem inconspicuous but wasn't sure if they bought it or not.

Ben looked at his wife and gave her a slight nod to show she could speak.

She shifted in her seat nervously. "Well, I heard that they had been murdered in these woods around that time. So sad. They were staying at the campground and their two sons..." They both looked up at us simultaneously, "...were left behind while they went missing. They were presumed to be dead after hours of searching the woods."

"Wow. We had no idea they were in trouble-"

Interrupting me, Ben said, "They weren't in trouble. It's just like she said. They went missing. Lots of things happen in these woods. Lots of things. Who knows what could've happened to them. Alligators, starvation, hypothermia, not to mention diseases like malaria and sepsis. We've been in these woods for a long time. We've seen it all."

Damian, like the numbskull he was, reiterated, "If you've seen it all, why didn't you see them? Do you know what happened to them?"

The couple stared at each other again. My heart rate skyrocketed, and the silence was overwhelming. I felt like if I let out a single breath, the entire house would cave in. I swallowed, staying perfectly still as we all stared at each other.

I finally interrupted, "Well, it seems that you don't have any additional information for us. We'll have to process this news together. So sorry to have bothered you." Damian wouldn't break eye contact with Ben. As I started to stand and prepared to leave, he stayed locked in. It was a chicken fight in the middle of a war. I so badly wanted to interrupt, but I couldn't stop the mysterious bond they had suddenly. It was like Damian had an intuition that I just didn't possess. He knew something that I didn't, and I wasn't sure he could even put it into words for me.

He stood up slowly, not breaking his stare. Ben slowly stood as well, his wife rising next to him, looking between the two of them just as I was. I didn't know what else to say; I had barely got out the last sentences, I couldn't breathe any longer. I grabbed Damian's right arm and began to walk towards the door. He waited until we were out of the kitchen to finally turn around and walk out with me.

As we walked down the front porch steps, Ben stood in the doorway.

"Goodbye, fellas. Have a nice walk, now."

He and his wife looked out the door as it slowly closed. We waited a moment to choose a direction so as to not alert them to our tent location. It was clear that they'd be watching us from the house.

"What was that?!" I yelled at Damian when we finally trekked back onto the path in the woods. "Why were you staring that guy down? We were doing just fine until you started to open up that big mouth of yours!"

He sighed, "Liam. You need to trust me. Something's not right with those people. We've never seen that place before, and yet it was here every summer we were? We've walked these woods! We know this place. And we know mom and dad. You think they would just walk off into the forest without telling us or anyone else where they were going?!"

"Well...no. But you can't just accuse people in their own homes. Especially in places we don't know. They could have beat you, or me. Or killed us! If they were involved somehow, what makes you think they would hold back from that?"

Damian thought about it as we continued our walk back to the campsite. He always held his head low when he felt guilty. I could tell he knew he had been wrong in this situation. He knew he'd made a mistake. He shouldn't have given up all of the information, even if he was just trying to help – eager to protect us and our parents. He was hot-headed, but growing up without parents, he needed to be. He needed to be confident, controlling over our surroundings. He had been responsible for me, constantly ready to fight anything that jeopardized our family.

When we finally reached our tent, he said, "I'm sorry. I should've thought it through. I just wanted to get the answers, and when he came at you like that...I don't trust them at all."

"I know. I don't either. Maybe Meredith knows something about them?"

"I wouldn't mind seeing her again." Damian winked at me.

Smirking at him, I punched his arm playfully. He pretended to be sore and laughed it off. It was getting dark by the time we got the fire started and set up for dinner. As we ate, we went over the facts again. Something was clearly off about that couple in the woods. We had honed our instincts during a lonely childhood. Damaged kids turn into damaged adults. When you've been frightened your entire life, everything seems threatening. So maybe the couple was just odd, older than we imagined, and going a little bit crazy.

We made jokes around the fire and attempted to lighten the mood, and then told ourselves that we would check in with Meredith in the morning since it was getting late. Sleep felt like a comfort I didn't deserve. Since our parents' death, I'd felt the responsibility of learning the truth. I was just better at ignoring it than Damian was, deciding to go about my life with that mystery unsolved.

Sleeping meant I wasn't working. Despite trying to avoid it for most of my life, the true weight of understanding what happened that night sat on my chest. I hadn't been able to breathe. Sleep came, but rest didn't.

5

I tossed and turned again, reliving the same moments. Breathless, stranded, alone, with no one but Damian to understand. The sirens, the lights, everything felt so real. I ran down that hill again, feeling each scrape and bruise form on my small body. I hit the bottom again, except this time it was hot. Hotter than I remembered. I smelled smoke, but not like a barbeque grill. Like a thick, black, smoldering smoke. And I heard my brother.

"LIAM!"

I turned to look for him, but I couldn't find him.

"LIAM!"

Again, I searched the woods for his familiar face.

I felt a shake this time and was suddenly awake, staring into my brother's terrified eyes. Smoke began to fill the tent. I grabbed my backpack as Damian grabbed his. Rushing to get out, I went to pull the zipper and burned my fingertips, dropping the metal clasp in an automatic reaction.

Damian headed to the back of the tent, took out his pocket knife from the side pocket of his bag, and began to rip at the tent fabric. It only took a few seconds before we were outside, each of us coughing up a lung. Damian ran to the nearest tree, leaning one arm against it, huddling down and throwing up into the bushes.

Unable to swallow, I opened my water bottle to begin sipping it when I saw a shadow in the woods. Watching. Lurking. I tried not to move, but at a moment's notice, it took off into the woods.

I bolted. Chasing it through the trees, I began swerving under and over lost branches and logs. I was determined not to let the shadow leave my sight. Whoever it was had wanted to watch us suffocate in there.

The shadow came to the hill I fell down as a child and began slowly jumping down, watching each step it took. I didn't take the same approach.

I threw myself into the air, falling just as I did the day my parents were declared dead in this very forest. I didn't see much as I was rolling down the 30-foot drop, but eventually my body crashed into his.

He was tumbling with me. My lungs felt like they were bursting into flames. But I found him and brought him down. As we hit the bottom we came apart, and at that moment, he darted through the bushes, heading for the river. It took me a moment to get up and convince my body to run, but I wasn't far behind him.

I burst through the pine branches in the bushes surrounding the river and scanned left and right. No one. Silence.

There was no way anyone would attempt to cross this river. It was too deep. Even if they were crossing the river, I would've seen them. I was angry. Angry that I had lost him. Angry that I didn't get any answers. Angry that my body was now wounded from a lousy attempt at capturing whoever was out to get us.

Sulking, I headed back to the camp. Bruised and beaten, I returned to see the entire tent engulfed in flames with Damian leaning against a tree.

I walked over to him.

"Woah. You look great," he smiled shakily at me.

"Damian, I saw someone."

His mood shifted. "Like the guy who did this?! Did you get him? Or at least rough him up? Because it definitely looks like he got a few hits in..."

"He must have started this. He was watching us from the trees over there, waiting for us to die. I chased him into the woods and then threw myself at him. I thought I finally had him, but he escaped, and when I went to look out by the river, I couldn't see him anywhere."

"Well, it is dark out. He probably hid somewhere. I know you're going to make me say it... you think it was ol' Ben giving us a message? He definitely didn't like his wife telling us about our parents or us poking around."

Fury filled my eyes. "If it was some kind of message, he better know that we know where to find him. And we're coming for him."

"Hey, the anger issues look better on me, buddy," Damian said with a smirk and nudged me on the shoulder.

We stared at the fire for minutes, in disbelief of our close call with the grim reaper. The inferno grew and then began to fade. It was almost dawn when a car pulled up.

Meredith rolled down her window and called out, "Well, look who it is. I knew trouble would follow you!"

"That you did," Damian shouted back.

Meredith got out of her car, looking at what was left of our campsite. Someone had called in the fire, which thankfully hadn't spread far. It had incinerated the picnic bench, tent, and almost reached our car but thankfully was stopped by the sand and lack of wood. The tent now sat in a pile of smoldering embers.

"What were you cooking so late?" Her sarcasm was evident.

I rolled my eyes. "We were sleeping."

"Leave the fire still hot? Sometimes the embers can still fly off and catch something if it's not completely out."

Damian, now exhausted and irritable, explained, "We put the fire out completely. Even put water on it. We woke up to something near the tent, trying to start the tent on fire. We couldn't even get out the front because the zipper was too hot. Had to cut open the back. Someone lit the tent on fire."

Meredith looked both puzzled and suspicious. She walked around the embers, squatted down next to the ash, and began poking a stick through the mess. Suddenly, her eyes widened.

"I think I found the culprit, boys. I'm not sure if this means anything to you, but here it is."

Wrapping a piece of clothing around her hand, she brought a small metal Zippo lighter to us. Engraved in the silver was one name, written in a cursive font. Thomas. I didn't know a single Thomas, but maybe our friend Ben did. Meredith glanced at the two of us, noticing the confusion and suspicion on our faces.

"You think Thomas did this to you? Do you know who that is?"

23

"We have no idea who Thomas is. But I'm telling you right now, we know who did this."

"Well, I'm glad you boys are okay. Let's go back to my office and talk."

6

Going back to Meredith's office was strange. We'd never been inside of a sheriff's office before, but this place was clearly not the norm. Only three desks sat inside a small square room, with one adjacent room for the sheriff. He had a cloudy glass door with his name on the front. Brickett.

We sat down in the two chairs seated next to her desk. She powered up her computer and sat there waiting. We glanced uncomfortably at one another.

"Oh! Would you guys like any water or maybe a pop or something?"

I raised my water bottle. "I think I'm okay."

Damian nodded in agreement. We basked in the uncomfortable silence until the computer finally turned on, and Meredith began to type.

"So, what did you say his name was again?"

"He told us his name was Benjamin. I don't know his wife's name, they never said. Didn't look like they had any kids or pets, just alone in that big house out in the woods.

Is it dark brown with maroon shutters? Victorian style. Have you seen it before?"

She thought for a minute. "I haven't... which is strange because I've walked those woods my entire life. Let me search for them. Aren't very many people in this town, so it probably won't be too long before I find them."

"Great," I said.

I looked over at Damian, who was staring straight at Meredith. I nudged him, and he quickly turned back to me. He'd never looked this way at a woman before. I'd seen him try harder than anyone I know to get a lady, but swooning? It just wasn't his thing.

He gave me big eyes and turned back to watch her slim fingers type on the keyboard. Her eyebrows narrowed down in focus as she scoured the database based on the descriptions we'd provided. She knew this was going to be a tough case. Deep down, she knew she wasn't going to find them. Someone who had lived in this little town for twenty years didn't know the people who said they've been here since 1998? Doesn't sound right.

She gave us a look of despair. "Sorry, boys. They aren't in here. But! I have an idea. That campground used to have a book with all the regular campers' names and phone numbers inside. It's a stretch considering they don't seem like the camping type, but if they lived nearby, maybe they wanted to be a part of it."

Damian and I nodded in agreement. Meredith got up and walked into the sheriff's office. Shadows peeked through the clouded glass. The two of us watched in anticipation. The voices got louder until finally, she walked out with a large hardcover book with 1995-2005 written on the cover. More aggressively than expected, she slammed it on the desk in front of her.

"Fellas. We've got them."

Damian looked at me confused, as I shared the same expression with him, then with Meredith. She slowly opened the book to a photo on the first page. My stomach churned, nausea running up the back of my throat. I had to swallow a few times to keep anything from rising up again. The hair on my arms stood up. Damian looked as white as snow.

Meredith, confused, asked, "Is that not the couple?"

"No, that is them. Exactly. This was from 1995?!" Damian asked.

Meredith nodded. Pictured in the old photo were the man and woman we saw in that house in the woods. The exact man and woman. Not a single thing was out of place: the mustache, the yellow dress, the tan skin with sunken eyes.

"So, what does that mean?" I looked at him, shivering.

He shook his head. "How should I know what it means?"

Under my breath, I murmured, "Ghost Whisperer."

"Alright, I said one thing, and now you think I'm some sort of magic man," he scoffed.

"Well. Could they just have really young faces? Maybe they age well."

Meredith looked closer at the photo, bringing it up to her face, "I don't think so, guys. The chances of someone looking the same when they're 25 and 50 seems unreal. Are you sure they look like this?"

"We're positive. That photo could have been taken yesterday." Confirmed Damian.

"So what are you saying? Are they ghosts?" I asked bluntly.

Meredith shook her head and then nodded. "I don't know. But I'm saying something is fishy around here."

Damian raised his eyebrows. "I knew something was off."

We all looked at each other, unsure of our next move. The idea didn't seem so absurd now that a third party was in on it, too. The photo was uncanny. It was, without a doubt, the couple from the woods. It was obvious what we needed to do, but I don't think any of us were jumping at the idea.

Reluctantly I said, "We have to go back there."

"What were you guys even doing in the woods?" Meredith asked, sitting down heavily behind the desk.

I had completely forgotten that Meredith didn't know about our parents. We had all gotten along so well, we didn't realize she was out of the loop.

"Well," Damian began, "our parents brought us here all the time when we were little. We'd stay in the campground a few weekends a year. One year while we were in the campground, they disappeared into the woods. It was late at night or early in the morning. We woke up to find them gone, the tent empty. We searched around for them for a while before I went and found someone who called the police. They searched the woods for days and never found them."

"Oh my gosh. That's terrible. I'm so sorry." She rested her hand on Damian's shoulder and gave me a sympathetic look. "How old were you?"

"I was eight, Damian was twelve."

"Wow. I can't believe you had to go through that. I've heard about this case. And they never found anything, right?"

Damian shook his head, "Never. And they declared them both dead a few weeks later. It was too difficult to continue searching. They said people have gone missing before. It's tough terrain out there."

"So what about this Benjamin guy?"

Damian retold the story of Ben and how he had reacted when we spoke to him about our parents. How strange it was that he would react in such a way and how similar they looked to their photos in that book. It seemed impossible.

"It's just too weird," he said after the recap. "Too much of a coincidence. They know something, and we need to find out what that is."

Meredith stared at us both hard before nodding solemnly. "Well, I think it would be best if I go along with you."

I was never one for ghost stories, and I didn't really believe in them. I didn't realize that Damian did until he mentioned it to me the day before. Ghosts were so abstract, seemingly unrealistic. I almost chuckled at the thought of "fighting a ghost." I didn't even know where we should begin.

7

W e grabbed something to eat late in the morning, and Meredith drove us back to our campsite. We dreaded going into those woods again, unsure what would transpire and creeped out by this eerie couple. They hadn't been very hospitable the first time and possibly set our tent on fire. Who's to say they wouldn't kill us when we returned?

As we started to pack our bags for the trek, Meredith grabbed her backpack from her trunk and swung it on her back.

"I don't think you should come with us," Damian exclaimed after a long silence. Meredith looked ready to argue back, but he continued, "If we believe these people truly are ghosts or some kind of eternal whatever, it could be dangerous."

She scoffed. "Danger is my job. I'm here to protect this place, and I'm going to do my job." As she spoke, she got right up in his face and didn't seem so small anymore. "And if you have a problem with that, you'll have to drag me out of the woods yourself."

0

Damian relented and motioned for her to walk ahead. We all started into the woods, and it was hauntingly quiet. For hours, we walked with barely a word spoken between us. The anticipation began to build as late morning turned into afternoon. The rhythm of our footsteps grew loud, and my heart began to race, the butterflies in my stomach turning sour as we rounded the cliffside by the river.

By the time we made it to the extravagant home, the sun was past the halfway point in the sky, hanging low on the trees. The house looked the same; not a single thing was out of place. We weren't sure where to start. We all stood in the yard staring at each other until I finally gathered the courage to look into a front window.

"It doesn't look like anyone is home. Maybe we should knock?" I suggested.

Meredith walked up to the large front doors and landed three subtle knocks into the wood. She stood there and waited expectantly. Damian stood behind her as I remained beside the window, peering in. Meredith knocked again. Three times, small clicks rang from the door.

Again, nothing. We all looked at each other and shrugged. No one was home, so we slowly walked around the left side, an area we hadn't checked out before. The back of the house was as pristine as the front, but the yard was still in shambles. This time, we noticed a small shed that looked oddly out of place.

The shed was small but modern, like it had been pre-made somewhere else and placed on this property. It was white and covered with a vinyl-like material, contrasting with the rest of the house. It was surrounded by long, unkempt grass with weeds braided into each other.

"What do you think is in there?" I asked the group.

Damian looked at me somberly. "I think we're about to find out."

When we reached the door, we noticed a small padlock on a chain. Meredith reached into her bag, pulling out a pair of bolt cutters. She twisted them around the chain and yanked them together, breaking the chain apart. It fell to the ground.

"That'll do it," Damian smiled.

As we walked inside, we noticed it wasn't dusty like an old shed that hadn't been touched in years. Someone had been here recently, but it was a pigsty, random yard tools (that clearly hadn't been used), and full totes stacked upon each other. Meredith took down the tote on top of the pile and opened it. Coughing from the dust inside, she pulled out a pack of old Christmas cards.

She kept digging into the box while Damian and I took inventory of the tools. Some were more worn than others. It seemed they had recently used a mallet, a rake, a shovel, and a few other tools. Their yard certainly looked like they didn't know how to use any of them. So what were they using these for?

"Hey, guys?" Meredith called us over.

She held up a photo. Two young boys sat in the same sitting room we had seen yesterday. There was a Christmas tree behind them, with presents placed neatly underneath. The boys looked to be about nine or ten years old. The back of the photo, in neat handwriting, stated, *Thomas and Jack Christmas 1993*.

Damian finally spoke up. "You think they had kids?"

"I don't know; they don't seem like the type. But then, I don't know who else's kids these would be...who would

32

have a picture of someone else's kids tucked away in a tote?"

"Thomas, man, I think we have your lighter," he tried to chuckle.

Meredith shrugged and snuck the square photo into her pocket. We searched the rest of the shack, but Meredith came up empty as decorations and unused cleaning supplies filled most of the bins. We only found some dead mice and more useless tools, and a lawnmower that clearly had not been taken out in decades. As we walked out defeated, something caught my eye along the tree line.

As Meredith and Damian chatted and walked back towards the house, I began to walk toward the tree line. I tried to find what was so different about this spot, until I finally found a break in the trees and felt my breath catch in my throat.

"You guys are going to want to see this," I yelled over to them, shakily.

They began to walk towards me and the lot behind the backyard. A line of brush and trees hid it away, but it was like something called me to it. Maybe my parents, like Damian had said. Perhaps they were telling me exactly where to go.

Behind that tree line, there was an empty lot, covered in dirt, with no trees or bushes or flowers. Nothing. Absolutely desolate. That wasn't what was terrifying. Out of the ground, in the back-most left corner of the lot, I saw it. I saw it and knew exactly what this was. A graveyard. The dirty bones stuck out starkly against the dark soil.

We looked at the vast distance between where we stood and where the bones ruptured out of the ground. If the size of this lot was any indication, there had to be tons of bones buried here. Now the tools in the shed made sense - they needed the shovel to bury the bodies.

I felt a chill as I realized these people had murdered my parents. There was no question about it in my mind. My stomach began to turn, my hands shaking. Meredith had to excuse herself so she didn't vomit. She was strong, but apparently not when it came to graveyards and buried bodies.

"This is horrifying," she choked, turning the other way.

"Aren't you a sheriff or something?" Damian asked, trying for humor to mask his shock.

"Sheriff's deputy. And I break up bar fights and do paperwork. I don't find dozens of dead bodies in some random person's backyard."

"What are the chances they aren't human?" Damian asked hesitantly. I glanced at him. We'd come all this way – he'd practically dragged me out here – but the look on his face told me he wanted to be wrong about this. As much as we wanted to know what happened to our parents, as long as we didn't, there was a bead of hope. But to me, the bones in the ground extinguished that hope.

Meredith gave him a look but didn't answer. None of us actually thought this wasn't a massive human graveyard.

"Why would they do this? If they're ghosts, I thought ghosts just haunted their old homes and moved ouija boards," I said. "How can they even kill someone...?"

Meredith finally collected herself and moved closer to us. "I don't know a ton about the ghost world, or spirits or whatever, but I have a feeling this isn't normal."

"It can't be. We'd have way fewer people in the world if they all murdered this many humans," Damian explained.

We were silent, contemplating. I felt a wave of sadness wash over me. Were our parents here, buried in this yard? We needed to do more research. Who were those boys, and why were their photos in a forgotten box in the shed? What happened to them? Were they buried here with my parents? Were they ghosts too?

We slowly made our way back up to the house. The three of us decided to return to the sheriff's station for the night and sleep for a few hours before beginning our research. Damian and I wanted to head back straight away to make sure we weren't walking in the dark, but Meredith wanted to see inside the house. Something about women makes them want to see everything for themselves, even though we already knew what was inside. We shrugged off our irritation and watched her pick the lock.

"Isn't this illegal without a search warrant?" Damian asked, but he shut up when she glared at him.

"Wow," she said, "this is nicer than I was expecting! They have great interior decorating, just a little outdated."

We walked through the sitting areas and went back to the kitchen again, Damian watching out the front door to make sure Ben and his wife didn't arrive early. Meredith wasn't thrilled with the tour and wanted to see the upstairs. I tried to convince her that it was too risky, but the stubborn woman pushed ahead despite my concern. She really would make a great partner for Damian. They were both bull-headed.

The upstairs had one long hallway with one room off to the right and the rest down the strip to the left. She immediately opened the door to the right and stared in shock. She let out a large gasp. I pushed her out of the way to see for myself. There was almost nothing in the room. An old bed and a dresser with an oval mirror above it.

"Meredith! You scared the hell out of me! What if there was something in there!"

"It was just so dusty. Ugh. No one's been in here for ages," she complained and scrunched her nose up in disgust.

"Are you guys okay?" Damian yelled from downstairs.

"We're fine! Your girlfriend is afraid of dust," I yelled back.

Even though we were far away, I could picture him saying 'she's not my girlfriend' under his breath. But Meredith only smiled slightly.

We began walking down the dimly lit hallway and stuck our heads in a few doors, two bathrooms, and one bedroom—all layered with dust, all small and unused. The master suite was the largest at the end of the hall. We entered the room and were surprised by the level of cleanliness. The other rooms were clearly unused, and I doubt they'd even been in them in years. This room was brightly colored with a large square rug patterned in faded reds and blues. The attached bathroom was also large but had only a tub, a toilet, and a sink.

"Do ghosts use the bathroom...?" I asked, but Meredith was staring at the bed.

It was freshly made with white linens. "Maybe, if they sleep, too," she said.

The room felt cold. A draft flowed through even though there weren't any windows open. The king-sized bed barely filled the room. As we walked around, we felt each piece of wooden furniture. Every piece was dark wood, antique-looking. Everything was old yet beautifully restored or taken care of well.

As we stood in the bathroom inspecting the blue tile, the lights flashed off. Confused and concerned, we yelled to Damian to see if something had gone wrong downstairs.

"Damian?!" I shouted, loud enough to hear through the large house. No answer.

I yelled again, "Damian!"

Again no answer. We rushed downstairs, and I ran ahead with Meredith trailing behind. As we both tumbled down the large staircase, we saw Damian. He stood in one of the sitting rooms, pressed against the wall, gasping for air.

As we drew closer, we saw his feet off the ground and his face starting to turn a shade of blue and purple. Unsure of how to help, I ran to him and began to pry the invisible hands around his neck. As I touched them, they came to life. A man's set of hands wrapped around my brother's neck. Meredith joined me in pulling the man off of Damian.

Fighting his beastly strength, we released Damian from his grasp. The hands flickered into sight, Ben's angry face briefly visible before disappearing again. Wind rushed past us, almost pushing us over. Damian fell to the ground, panting and pulling air into his lungs. He grabbed at his throat as if to make sure there weren't still hands around it. I grabbed his arm and pulled him to his feet as we flew out the front door and into the nearby woods. We hid in the trees for a few minutes, watching and waiting for someone to come out and try to find us, but no one followed.

Damian was shaken but had enough strength to make the walk back. Bruises lined his neck. They were hot to the touch, and he continued to raise his fingers to them. He claimed he'd be okay with some painkillers and ice packs, but I could tell the entire thing rattled him. Jumpy and scared, we trudged through the woods.

"I guess that explains how they can harm people," Meredith whispered as we hurried down the trail.

We made a fire as soon as we returned to camp. It was starting to get dark. Damian began to cook some burgers as we talked through our thoughts.

"I just can't wrap my mind around this. They are actually ghosts," I started, "I mean, I'm going, to be honest, I never believed in them."

Meredith sighed. "I never say never anymore. Anything can happen, things that are real seem surreal. So why can't things we've never believed in before exist?"

"I always knew." Damian was staring into the fire, the bruises looking especially ghastly in the firelight.

"Damian, you never knew. Come on. I know I joke about you being a ghost whisperer, but you can't actually believe you can talk to ghosts."

Damian turned toward the two of us, his face serious. "Of course I did. I told you, mom and dad have talked to me before. Not...explicitly, but they've given me inklings before. I know it was them, I could feel it."

"Do you think that was your heart, or your parents?" Meredith asked, fully engaged with him.

"I know it was them. It's like they whispered in my ear, but I couldn't hear it. I would just think things and didn't know how my thoughts got there. My skin would get cold, and I would feel dad put his arm around my shoulders. There were ways I could tell."

In shock, I blurted out, "I didn't realize that was happening to you. How come you never told me about it before?"

"Well, it didn't seem like it was time."

I felt terrible that Damian believed he couldn't open up to me about his thoughts. But as a man who didn't believe in ghosts before that day, I understood why he wouldn't say anything to me until he had a push to do something about it. I would have laughed at him or written off his experiences.

"That's very brave of you to share." Meredith smiled at him.

He raised his eyebrows. "I'm extremely brave." Ah, there was the usual Damian.

"I like men who are brave."

"I like women who know what they like."

I felt as if I had walked into a room I wasn't supposed to be in. As much as I wanted them to get together, I didn't want to be in the middle of their flirtatious banter. They stared at each other for far too long, until I finally chimed in.

"Damian, I'm no chef, but I think your burgers are almost burnt."

We sat and ate together. Meredith told us about her parents and her childhood growing up in Atlanta. Her brothers were both younger and working in her hometown. She missed them all so much, but she couldn't get enough of the countryside. Nature called to her, and you could see it in her eyes. She seemed so at home sitting on a log, her boots planted in the dirt.

"Should we get going?" I asked.

"Yeah...I'm just, are you sure it's okay?" Damian asked.

Meredith nodded. "Come to the station. We can sleep there for a bit and then get to work on figuring out how to destroy these ghastly beings and put an end to this."

8

We piled into Meredith's car and drove back to the station. It wasn't long before we were all dead asleep, laying on spare blankets taken from the lost and found.

For a few hours, in my dreams, it felt like nothing had happened. Everything was okay, I was safe, Damian was safe. As I awoke, an empty feeling dropped in the pit of my stomach. Reality jolted me from my slumber. The truth was that I wanted to learn what had happened to my parents. I wanted to understand how to be rid of this demon couple that seemed to want our entire family dead now that we were hunting them down.

Awake before us, Damian brought me coffee. An unusual turn of events since I was usually the one up first in the real world.

"Have trouble sleeping?" I asked him.

"I think I got a few minutes in there."

I turned his head up with my fingers to see if the marks had worsened, and they had. His neck sported large purple bruises on each side in the shape of fingers. I winced at the sight and removed my hand from his jaw.

"I'm so sorry we left you alone down there."

He shrugged it off. "Glad I could take one for the team. It looks worse than it is."

"Well, we should've been there sooner. Or done something differently. You could've died..."

"But, I didn't," he interjected, sitting.

"I know. It's a good thing you didn't because it's all hands on deck today. Shall we get to work? What do we do about sleeping beauty?"

I pointed over at a heavily breathing Meredith, rolled up in an oversized comforter. Her body was splayed out across the ground with her back to the floor.

"Eh, she'll join us eventually. Let her sleep in a bit longer."

"You're just saying that because you like her," I winked at him. He gave a knowing shrug as if to say, *Can you blame me?*

We began our work online, diving into forums. We came across many who talked about spirits as peaceful or harmless. Obviously not the ones we were working with. Most of them had techniques to talk ghosts through their pain, allowing them to move on—nothing on the evil spirits and how to rid the world of their terror.

As we continued to research, Meredith woke up to some hot coffee made by none other than Damian. She started to explore the family, and slowly but surely, she uncovered the whole story.

"Come read this."

Damian leaned over her shoulder and read out loud, "February 20th, 1994, The Sonora Sonet. Over the harsh winter storm last month, four bodies were discovered in a home in the woods near Sonora Park. The Lindum family lived in a small vacation home in the park during the holiday season. The only entry and exit to the property are trails through the forest. The bodies of two adults, Benjamin and Abigail Lindum, were found in their bed, trapped in their small home in the middle of the park. The cause of death was deemed hypothermia. Two children were also discovered with evidence of cannibalism to their bodies. Investigation into the children is ongoing."

Sitting back, we all fell silent. What a terrible way to go, hypothermia in your own home. Slowly turning into monsters until you eat your own children. But you still die in the end. Just awful.

It was then that I remembered my parents. They killed my family, took them from us. Stripped us of our childhood just because they felt guilty. Is that what kept them on this side of the world? They couldn't bear to go on and see the children they had sacrificed?

"Well, that would definitely cause some unfinished business." Damian broke the silence. "I feel like this is why our parents have been reaching out to me. They want us to put an end to this."

I slowly nodded. "As much as I don't want to do this, I believe you. I think we need to figure out how to make them finally leave the human world, or that graveyard will just keep growing."

"Is this even possible? I've never heard of ghosts eating people." Meredith said, puzzled.

We didn't know enough about the ghost world. We continued to research online, sipped our coffee, and pored over blog posts, articles, and forums.

"Look here!" Damian exclaimed. "This post talks about how a ghost can be condemned to devour human corpses because of the evil deeds they have committed on earth. I think eating your own children might count."

"This is terrifying!" gasped Meredith as she read over his shoulder. "Does it say how to release them from their sins? Send them onward?"

"Unfortunately, no. We'll keep searching." Damian sighed.

We were coming up empty until finally I pulled up an old thread of questions on a forum that were similar to ours. How do you get rid of an evil spirit who just won't go?

On this thread, we uncovered a ritual to get rid of a ghost using the bones from their Earthly bodies. Supposedly, if you salted them and set them on fire, it would set the spirits free. This method sounded easy enough. But there was one problem - we didn't know where to find their bones, and returning to that house in the forest seemed risky.

"What is the likelihood that they are buried on the property? Maybe we can go through the woods to the backyard again, and they won't even see us?" Damian suggested.

Meredith glanced at him, annoyance written on her face. "They'll definitely be on the lookout now. They tried to kill you yesterday, or did you forget about that already?"

"I didn't forget, I just thought maybe we could make it work. They didn't see us back there the last time!" he defended.

I frowned. "What if we come prepared? Maybe if we lay a circle of salt around the bones first, since it seems like salt is important here. And then we can salt each body in the graveyard and burn it. That could work if we went fast?"

Meredith considered the idea, chin in hand. "It could work, but still kind of risky. It seems like a bit much, we'd need a lot of salt, and we'd have to move quickly. Plus, it would take a long time to burn all of those bodies."

We contemplated it some more, tossing out a few ideas here and there but ultimately coming up empty-handed. Feeling defeated, we grabbed our gear and set out to execute my original idea. We stopped at the local gas station and general store, grabbing all of the salt they had in stock, and by mid-day, we were walking through the forest again. Damian had been awfully quiet and clearly had something on his mind.

"If we don't make it through this, I want you guys to know that you're the people I want to spend my last hours with."

Shocked by his sincerity, I responded, "You're the people I want to be with, too."

Meredith furrowed her brow and looked back and forth between the two of us. "I don't want either of you talking about dying, you hear? That's not a good start to this trip. You should know better."

An uncomfortable silence passed until she finally continued, "But if it was our last day here, I would like to say it was great to meet the both of you."

We smiled and nodded at her in thanks. It had been a wild journey so far. To think that just two days ago, I was sitting in my kitchen making coffee for my sleeping brother. Now I knew way too much about ghosts and how to free their spirits. The strangest part was that I felt comfortable with it. Even scared out of my mind, I felt determined to return to that house and execute this mission.

It was like I finally made it to where I was supposed to be. I was supposed to be here. Destined, or something like that. Damian felt it too, I could tell by his confident walk and ability to be calm. We were all comfortable. With each other, with our investigation, with our abilities against these creatures. We were doing what we were supposed to be doing. It felt strangely perfect.

"When we get there, we should walk around back and slip into the graveyard. We have to be quick and quiet; we don't really know what they're capable of. They could sense us coming or be ready for us."

Damian and Meredith nodded. "Agreed." They spoke in unison.

"Damian, you have the salt. Let's each hold on to one, just in case. If anyone gets separated from the group, scream and draw a salt circle around you. I don't think the woman, Abigail, will come after us. She seemed pretty meek around her husband, but anything can happen, so be on guard."

They nodded as the house came into view, and we craned our necks to try and see inside from so far away. The windows were clean but old and had a greyish filter on them. Damian stood on the outer edge and stopped every once in a while to check the windows and doors again. If anything moved, he would motion for us to stop. But it only happened once - he thought he saw a curtain move by a fraction inside. We all froze, not wanting to risk anything. We paused briefly before deciding we were safe to continue.

As we entered the backyard, past the shed, and into the graveyard, we began salting the area in a large circle. Damian, our guard, looked up at the house, quickly turned to us, and yelled, waving his arms frantically.

Meredith and I looked up from our salt paths to find Ben staring at us with wide eyes through a window. His anger was evident. We sped up quickly, running and laying as much salt as we possibly could. As we both glanced up, we saw Ben as he floated through the walls of the house (something I'd only seen in movies) and raced over to the graveyard.

His suit blew in the wind, the fabric billowing against him. The air grew colder the closer he got. He turned increasingly pale and hollow as he raced toward us. Our hearts began to skip as we ran around the circle, ensuring we had done every step correctly. As we threw the last bit of salt on the circle, he came down to the ground outside of the graveyard.

"WHAT DO YOU THINK YOU'RE DOING HERE?!" he screeched.

"Saving this town from your terrors. We know what you are and what you did," Damian spoke with zeal.

Ben gave a laugh that had an undertone of evil, his eyes glinting. "OH. Do you?!"

Meredith stepped forward, close to the inner edge of the circle. "Thomas and Jack? What happened to them?"

"I think if you knew, you wouldn't have come back here," he turned his head to the side, giving us a smile with dead eyes.

I finally got the courage to speak up. "You ate them. Your own children. How could you do that? You killed them!"

Ben didn't look at all fazed by my declaration. "Why yes. If you knew the answer to the question, why did you even bother to ask?!" He leaned as far as he could toward the circle surrounding us, eager to get to us.

His face emptied of emotion as he stood larger. His body began expanding, taller than the trees, standing over us as if an invisible bubble was the only thing keeping us safe.

"Why did you kill them?!" I shouted up at him, my neck almost at a 90-degree angle.

He faked a few cries, mocking me. *"Why did you kill them?* Boohoo. We needed them. We were dying, we were going to die, and they saved us. They were given to us to be sacrificed."

He began to shrink, standing only at about seven feet tall now, but still stalked the edge of the circle.

Damian spoke quietly to keep the ghost calm and hopefully small. "But you died. And you're dead now anyway. So what was the point of murdering your innocent children? And why do you keep killing?" He gestured around him at the graveyard.

"Enough about the children. What about you. Why are you here?" He began to grow again in his anger. "Why have you come back again and again to torture us?!"

"The Sullivans - that couple with the two boys? You killed them," Damian yelled.

"Maybe. Maybe not. Can't remember everyone you kill," Ben shrugged.

"So you've killed many?" Meredith asked.

He looked at her, surprised by her strong voice, "Why yes, I have, little lady."

"And why is that?" her voice sounded innocent, curious.

He laughed at her. "You're not as innocent as you sound. You, too, are evil inside. Everyone is."

We began to pick through the shallow graves, hurrying to find bones before the soil devoured the salt, and we were stranded. He sat patiently, mocking us, waiting for his moment to strike. His head stayed cocked to one side, with an empty smile a seat for his mustache.

"Why?! Why are you doing this?!" he mocked. *"No! Stop! Oh no! You'll find us!"*

Glancing at each other, we realized we weren't going to be able to find their bones among so many others. We didn't want to destroy all of the evidence, either. We began to dig up each grave, taking one bone from each and leaving the rest, creating small piles and then moving on. One by one, we salted and burned the piles. Ben still chuckled to himself, pacing the edge of the circle and taunting our hectic work. We tried, but by the time we all huddled around the last grave and lit the bones, he was still laughing.

"They must have them hidden," I whispered to Damian and Meredith.

"Wait." Meredith looked down, concentration drawing her brows together. "Remember when we went inside and toured the place? And I looked at all of those photos in their tubs in the storage shed? There's a very particular chest. It's in their bedroom. Before Damian screamed, I saw it in the corner by a reading chair when we were upstairs. I thought it was just a chest, but in the Christmas photo...they used it to store the kids' toys. Why would they keep that if they wanted to stop thinking about the kids? They've gotten rid of everything their kids' had. The only reason they'd keep that chest is if they wanted to hide something inside."

Damian and I looked at each other and nodded. Meredith sounded sure of herself. We had nothing to lose. The only problem now was how to get up to the house - how to get past Ben.

Damian spoke first and quietly. "Anyone have a plan?"

We looked over at Ben, who was no longer watching us but still pacing. He seemed content to wait us out.

"What if we just went past him? Went backward, into the brush?"

Meredith reminded me, "You saw how fast he got over here. Once he realizes we're gone, we'll be dead. Plus, we don't know where Abigail is. We can't even take on one, much less both of them."

"Alright. I have an idea," I said.

A minute later, while Ben was turning to gaze around the property, Meredith and Damian flanked right and left. At the same time, I stood back into our safe circle and covered the rest. In one swift movement, we had him trapped.

In the seconds he had his eyes off of us, we had encapsulated him in a salt circle, covering the ground around him with a thick white line. As he finally realized he had been tricked, he grew as tall as he could. Almost 15 feet tall he stood, larger than the trees but trapped inside of his circle. He released a thunderous roar, louder than anything I'd heard before. It shook me to my core. We left the safety of our circle and ran to the house as he screamed behind us.

The door squeaked shut as we entered and turned on the dim lights of the first floor. Staking out the first floor, we carefully walked around the kitchen, sitting areas, downstairs bathroom. Checking the backyard periodically to make sure our giant was still contained – he was.

"Where do you think she is?" I asked.

"I don't know," Damian replied, "but we need to keep an eye out for her."

We slowly walked up the stairs. Meredith and I checked the first room - no luck. Nothing had changed. Damian and I checked each side of the hallway, opened doors simultaneously, and communicated that they were clear. Only one door remained, and we weren't sure if she would appear to us or not.

As we grew closer to the door, we heard a low moan. Each step we took seemed to make it grow in agony. The outpouring of grief from Abigail became more and more apparent. We didn't have a plan as we entered the room, which scared us.

Damian opened the door slowly, the three of us standing in the large doorway looking in. In her yellow dress, Abigail sat on the floor, strewn across the wooden chest we believed the bones were in. Her screams and low aching moans were louder than ever, shaking the floorboards. You could feel the grief in the pit of your stomach, like a growing ball of bad energy.

"Abigail?" Meredith asked, stepping into the room tentatively.

Abigail turned toward us, a hopeful smile on her face and tears streaming down her face. "Yes?"

"I'm Meredith. It's really nice to meet you."

Abigail tilted her head to the side slowly. A tear fell from her right eye and dripped down her cheek. She sat there for too long. Long enough for all of us to look at each other, in fear and confusion, then back at her.

Snapping her neck back into place, she said, "It's so nice to meet you too. Who are you?"

"I'm Meredith. We're here to help you." She gestured at the two of us.

"You brought friends?" she asked, crawling a bit closer to us.

"I'm Damian, and this is Liam."

I nodded, bending down slowly to the floor so as to not startle her. She didn't seem to remember us at all.

She giggled, another tear rolling down her cheek. "Nice to meet you."

Meredith slowly lowered herself down, speaking on the same level as Abigail. "Are you upset today?"

Taken aback, she responded, "No. Why would you say that?"

"We heard some crying from the hall. Are you alright?"

Abigail touched her cheek and felt the damp skin. Surprised, she said, "I guess I am."

I leaned in a bit closer. "Do you know why you're so upset?"

She looked back at the chest on the floor, pulling herself towards it. "This. My children. They're gone. It's all my fault."

She whimpered and drew the chest back into her, curling her arms around it. Her legs went limp behind her as if she had no more strength from the grief.

"It's alright..." she sniffled, "Ben should be home soon...I should...get started on dinner. We have to eat tonight or..."

As she got up to leave the room, she stood in the doorway, looking off into the distance. Meredith turned to face her, still sitting on the ground. "Or what, Abigail?"

"Or Ben will be angry. And we'll have to leave."

"Leave where?" Damian asked.

"Leave here."

Meredith chimed in as Abigail was about to close the door, "Why do you need to eat to stay here? What is it that you have to do?"

"Eat more. Continue eating. Always eating."

"What are you eating tonight?" I asked.

Abigail finally looked down at us, cocked her head with a confused look and answered, "Why, campers, I suppose. That's what Ben usually brings home. Maybe I'll get lucky and he'll bring me some locals. They taste sweeter," she giggled and closed the door on her way out.

9

"So, they eat to survive on Earth?" Damian asked.
Meredith kept her eye on the door.
"Sounds like it. Ben is the monster. She sounds like a sweet and tortured soul."

"Sweet?" I asked. "Eating my parents was the kind thing to do?"

"That's not what I meant, and you know that. I just mean she doesn't seem like she wants to stay here, to continue doing this. There must be two sides to her - one when she's with Ben and one when she's alone."

I nodded. Abigail was clearly under the spell of her husband, the controlling psycho maniac who tried to murder us.

The three of us turned our attention to the chest in front of us. As we pushed it open, a horrible smell wafted out into the room. Damian pulled up his shirt to use it as a face shield; I plugged my nostrils with my fingers, and Meredith had to physically walk away to not throw up her lunch. Damian began to look through the bones to make sure there were multiple bodies inside.

He began to match up different femurs, finding at least three different pairs and setting them aside. As we sorted through the mess, Meredith sat in the corner closest to the door to avoid the smell. We attempted to separate them, but we were no anatomy experts, so it was difficult. We decided not to waste time and began to create a place to burn them all together, dousing them with our remaining salt.

We filled the bathtub with a layer of water and discovered a large metal bucket in the corner. As we carried the bucket out of the bathroom, Meredith screamed.

The hair on our necks stood. The lights flickered above us, and the ground shook.

We turned to find Meredith pinned on the ground by an angry Abigail. She had her hands on Meredith's shoulders as Meredith flailed her legs, trying to fling the ghost off. As we ran to help, Abigail turned and looked at us. We were both flung back and hit the wall by the door.

Barely able to move from Abigail's power, Damian and I attempted to stand but were unsuccessful. Struggling to get up, we looked at each other in defeat. The feeling arose in me again of being buried, unable to breathe. My heart raced, the floor becoming sand I was unable to move in. My lungs collapsed inside of me from my body pushing against a force much stronger than my own.

Abigail threw her head back towards Meredith, staring into her eyes. Meredith tried to shut hers and moved her head from side to side. Abigail concentrated, and Meredith's head turned back toward her.

"HOW COULD YOU DO THIS ME!" she screamed into Meredith's face, less than an inch away from her.

Meredith managed to keep her eyes closed as she wailed, "Do what?!"

Abigail had her hands out before us, trapping us where we were. The weight was almost unbearable, and I could hear Damian struggling to breathe as much as I was.

"YOU...YOU...MY HUSBAND IS TRAPPED. YOU SAID YOU WERE MY FRIEND!"

"Abigail, I am your friend. I'm trying to free you, reunite you with your children!"

She got even closer to Meredith's face. "I just want to be with my husband," she whispered into her ear.

With an angry cry, Abigail let the two of us free and pushed Meredith's body into the side wall, smacking her face as she whipped her around. She looked larger now, taller than each of us, and she crawled in a squatting position as if to get closer to our faces. Eye contact seemed important to her, to look into our souls and determine who she was going to kill.

As she let go of Meredith, she shifted her focus to lifting me into the air against the wall. She screeched as loud as she could, ambling closer. Damian covered his ears, doubling over in pain from the sound.

She eyed me, getting too close for comfort. I turned my face to the side, and she snapped it back forward, causing me to let out a painful grunt. Damian came up behind her, whacking her in the head with a metal pipe from the bathroom. It distracted her long enough for her to drop me to the floor. I heard a snap and felt a burning pain shoot up my ankle. She now fixated on Damian, chasing him into the bathroom with a manic smile.

He tripped over the bathtub and fell, landing hard on the outer edge. Lifting her hands, she flung his head into the side of the tub and then abruptly turned around, screaming in pain. Her body became pale, small, and slowly drifted away.

Damian peeked his head out of the bathroom, blood running down the side of his face from a large gash. I turned around, still on the floor and gripping my ankle, to find Meredith standing with a burning bone in her hand.

I stood and limped over to her. In shock, she stood facing the bathroom door, still looking where Abigail had stood.

I gently took the bone from her hand and threw it into the tub. One by one, we burned the bones to ensure they were all able to leave. As we finished, we stared at each other for a moment, speechless, proud of what we had overcome and accomplished.

We sat together on the front porch waiting for backup for Meredith and local police detectives. We were all exhausted. Meredith seemed still troubled by something. I don't know if she was happy about having to force Abigail to leave.

While we waited, Meredith confirmed, "I feel bad for her. She was so nice."

"She was," Damian responded.

"Why did she come back for us? For him?"

I imagined what would happen if my father had left my mother. Would she have gone after him? He wouldn't have ever left her, they were so happily in love. But if he had left, I liked to think she would follow. She would chase her love. She was motivated to keep the family together, planning fun game nights. Camping trips were always her idea. My father wasn't Ben. I couldn't imagine chasing after a man who forced you to eat your own children to stay alive. He was a whole other monster.

"Have you ever had a friend that keeps going back to a man she doesn't belong with? That's what it's like."

Damian was right. People like Ben stuck their claws into others. They captured them with charm and then forced them to stay when things got bad.

"I guess so," she sighed.

"Sometimes, it's just time for people to go. Even if it's not peacefully."

She nodded slightly.

I tried to lighten the mood. "Hey. You saved us in there. You helped us escape, and otherwise, we could have died. One more hit to the head, and Damian could've been a goner. You were an equal part of everything we accomplished. The research, that fight back there, the theories, everything. You were there for all of it. And we did a good thing back there."

She smiled, sat up, and hugged me. The police and paramedics arrived. They must have had to figure out a way in from the forest, having taken quite a while. Damian helped me up, and we walked off of the porch and out to the paramedics.

They checked us out while the police searched the property and asked us questions. They cleared the house and the shed and announced no one was present. We pointed them to the graveyard. We had decided not to tell them the full story. We would sound crazy, and they would never believe us.

They taped off the area and began documenting and photographing the scene. By now, the sun was long past the horizon, and we were standing in the cold, illuminated by the artificial lights erected around the scene. We were removed to get checked at the small hospital in town. They discharged us quickly with only a few scrapes and a brace for my ankle.

Meredith drove us back to our campsite, where the only thing we had left was our truck. Proud of our work, we stood outside for a few minutes staring at the mess of ashes. The sun began to rise. It felt strange to be finished, to have accomplished our extremely crazy goal. To avenge our parents and save the entire community. We made sure that no one would need to be afraid of these woods again. And we were good at it, it made us feel happy and proud.

"So what now?" Meredith asked us.

"Well, I guess we'll go home and figure that out. What are your plans?" Damian questioned.

She thought about it. "I will have a lot of paperwork to complete after this one. And I have some business to take care of in the city."

I was hoping that by business in the city, she meant visiting us. You don't have a night like we did and never see each other again. The weekend had been life-changing, everything shifted. We had to keep in touch. We were the only ones who would understand.

"Oh, do you?" Damian smirked.

"I do. There are some people there that I like, that I think I need to see," she smiled.

"Well then, I guess we'll see you there."

"Maybe you will."

She got back into her car as Damian watched her drive off. He smiled at the thought of her coming into the city for him. That strong woman had him wrapped around her finger, and she knew it.

"I felt them," he said after her taillights disappeared.

"Who? Mom and dad?" I asked.

"Yeah. I felt them say goodbye. They told me they were proud of us. That we did a good job. That we finally set them free. They were really happy to go."

He smiled a genuine smile and chuckled a bit. Looking at him made me chuckle too. Our work here was done. We had done it all for them, and they were proud and finally released to the beyond. I couldn't imagine sharing a better moment with the one person I loved the most in the world.

"Shall we?" I asked, gesturing to the truck.

"We shall."

10

On the car ride home, we listened to music and watched the sunrise. As we entered the city, I invited Damian to stay with me in the apartment. At least until he knew where he was going next. He still didn't have a job and didn't know what to do from here. And, to be honest, neither did I. Before all of this, I worked at a desk job in bookkeeping. It all seemed so insignificant now.

The police called a few weeks later and informed both Damian and me that they found over twenty different corpses in the backyard. They identified almost all of them with carbon testing and possible time matches, including our parents. We had helped solve over twenty missing person cases from the area. It was crazy to think about.

The weight of our parents' death seemed to be lifted off of our shoulders. We didn't feel bogged down by the unknown. I didn't miss the panic attacks or gasping for air in my sleep. I didn't seem to mind remembering Abigail's face running at me, or Ben grasping my brother's neck because they were no longer here. We conquered them, we beat them. They weren't going to terrorize us any longer.

I never had those nightmares again, but sometimes I would see my parents in my dreams smiling at me. Proud of who they raised, who my brother raised, who I became. I was proud to be me and to have a brother who talked me into something so insane and so liberating. I couldn't stop thinking about that weekend.

One day, Damian entered the kitchen and put his head in his hands just as he had done before our trip. I knew immediately that something was up. He stared at the counter and said nothing.

"What's up this time?" I asked with a sigh.

"Nothing, nothing...it's just. I think I figured out what I want to do," he shrugged, playing with his coffee cup on the countertop.

Intrigued, I asked, "Oh? Do you?"

"I do. I would like to do what we did for mom and dad."

Confused, I asked, "What do you mean? We already did that. We can't do it twice?"

"I know, I know. I mean, do what we did for mom and dad, but...for other people."

"You want to become the ghost whisperer?" I joked.

He shrugged. "I want to figure out what happened. Lots of people go missing or turn up dead, and no one takes the time to find out what actually happened. Does it always involve ghosts? No. But sometimes it does, and that's where I come in. Come on, you can't tell me you haven't been thinking about it."

I had been thinking about it. A lot. So much in fact that I had already created a business and applied for a private investigator license so we could officially charge clients. I had been dropping clues to Damian for weeks. Talking about how much fun we had, how good we were at it, and how good it felt that we accomplished something so great. I was just waiting for it to be his idea, for him to ask me to join him.

"I have been thinking about it. The business license came in yesterday."

He stood abruptly, shocked. "Are you kidding me? You've been planning this for weeks?"

"I knew as soon as we got home that we needed to do something like this," I smiled.

He dug through the pile of mail and found the paperwork. Staring at the papers in his hands, he shuffled through them, tearing up.

"You named it, 'Whisper Investigations'?"

"I did. It fits, don't you think?"

He laughed. "It really does."

With a smirk, I turned toward him, "Remember that summer camp we went to in middle school?"

"Uhm...Yeah, I guess." He wiped his tears away and shot me a confused look.

"A boy mysteriously died there a few years after we stopped going," I mentioned nonchalantly.

His eyebrows shot up. "Maybe we should talk to some of his family."

"Maybe I already did."

II

11

The sound of sprinting footsteps echoed through the empty mess hall. The small girl's breathing was labored, she had pains in her sides from running, but she couldn't stop. She was crying as she limped towards the door, throwing her weight into the heavy wooden joint and forcing herself forward. She stumbled, fell hard upon the graveled path, but could not afford to linger for long. Scrambling back to her feet, the small girl lurched forward, launching herself into the wooded trail, ducking beneath trees and dodging branches. She screamed for help, but there was no point. No one could help her.

As she escaped the trees and found herself at the edge of the water, she tripped a second time, hitting the earth bodily. Her fingers grasped at dry leaves and wet soil, trying to find the strength to pull herself up again, but exhaustion overwhelmed her. She tried to crawl, to keep going, but a cold, clammy hand had grasped her ankle. She screamed and dug her nails into the earth to anchor herself, but it was futile. Her bloodcurdling scream echoed across the quiet lake as she was dragged violently down beneath its depths. Then, as the cold water covered her face and filled her lungs, I screamed myself awake.

12

I yelped as I took notice of my surroundings, slowly realizing that I was in a warm car with my brother, who was looking at me with worry and confusion.

"What? What!?" Damian asked, looking at me and then back to the road. "Do I need to pull over?"

"No," I said quietly. "No, it's nothing. Just a bad dream."

I eased back into my seat, though still feeling uneasy. I thought back to my nightmare, dwelling on how vivid it all seemed. The woods, the lake, the girl...the girl. Everything about her seemed so lifelike and familiar. Everything that had happened to her in the dream, I had felt too. I lent an uneasy hand down to my ankle, almost expecting to find moisture there from the wet, clammy hand of whatever had dragged the girl beneath the surface of the water.

My fingers brushed gingerly against the skin, finding no mysterious marks there. I breathed out a sigh of relief, something that Damian noticed.

"I saw a sign advertising a motel up ahead. Let's stop there for the night. Rest up before we get to Camp Hollyfalls. You good with that?"

I nodded, not really in the mood to argue. I didn't know what I would have rather done; all I knew was that I wanted to shake this feeling of dread. Yet, every time I blinked, I saw her. I saw her body suspended in that dark water, hair in dark clouds hovering around her face. Her mouth open, screaming in vain as no sound came up to the surface, only angry bubbles escaping her mouth.

As the car came to a stop at the motel, the expression on my face was blank. The yellow neon was flickering in places as the lighting died out. The sign had once shone brightly as 'The Roachell Motel,' but as different letters had gone out, the sign simply read —

"Roach Mol," I read aloud, looking over at Damian with a smirk.

"Hey, it's a place to sleep. Better than nothing," Damian said before he lifted himself out of his seat and walked over to the main office. I got out of the car as well, but not to join him. Instead, I inhaled deeply as I pressed my back against the car, staring up at the midday sky. All of my days seemed to blend together as of late. Since Damian decided that we should go into business together and begin Whisper Investigations, the two of us had spent countless hours getting everything in order. Damian took care of most legal and technical aspects; licenses, permits, securing gigs. This little expedition was his doing, after all. He was the one who had decided to investigate the deaths at Camp Hollyfalls, not me. If I'm honest, I'm still not even entirely sure I want to do paranormal investigations, but if it helps people? Damian seems to think it will, so, I mean, what else have I got?

Damian came out of the office at that moment, the screen door banging behind him as he walked towards me, dangling the room key out in front of him before dropping it into my hand.

"That's your key, so don't lose it. Guy said it's a $75 replacement fee, and I am not paying for that – so don't lose it!"

"I got it. I got it...jeez," I said as Damian pointed us in the direction of our room. I grabbed our duffels from the car and followed him to room eighteen, which looked just about what I expected from "Roach Mol." The two double beds that took up most of the room had the same mustard yellow bedspreads with ugly green embroidery. There was only one window in the room, and the view was blocked by an AC unit that looked like it belonged in a museum; large, clunky, and barely chilled the air.

"Claimed!" Damian exclaimed as he leaped onto one of the beds, kicking off his shoes. I couldn't help but give a small smile at his antics. Despite everything we had gone through, he was still my brother.

"Let's get a quick nap in before we do any work," Damian said. Then he laid out on his bed and immediately flipped onto his stomach, and buried his face in his pillow.

I was apprehensive, as I was still a bit shaken from my earlier nightmare. However, as I sat upon my bed and found it deceptively comfortable, I gave in. I peeled off my shoes and slid under the covers, hoping for some well-deserved rest.

13

As soon as I closed my eyes, I drifted off to sleep, and my dreams began to weave before me. I found myself sitting on a sandy beach. The sun was shining, and there were children in swimsuits laughing and splashing while a few adults sunbathed on the shore. I looked curiously at them all, noting how odd their clothing was; everyone was wearing a swimsuit that looked like old pajamas. I had seen people dress like this for the beach before, but only in antique photographs. I tried to listen in on some of the conversations, but the words sounded garbled. It was as though I were hearing them talk through a barrier.

Suddenly, there was screaming and frantic calls for help, and I looked over to the water's edge and saw a little boy trying to keep his head above water. I sprang to my feet to help, but as soon as I stood, everyone disappeared. I glanced around, but now I was the only one on the beach. I scratched my head in confusion and took a few steps closer to the water, trying to make heads or tails of what happened, when a garbled voice came from behind me.

I spun around in time to see a teenage girl in a bikini looking up at me through massive bug-eyed sunglasses. I could not make out what she said, as her words were as distorted as everyone else had been, but by her demeanor, I guessed she wanted me out of her sun. I took a few steps back and watched as she returned to reading her magazine, which featured a blonde model with short hair and thick mascara. The scene was relatively peaceful, but that did not last long. Two teenage guys ran up to the lounging girl, their voices sounding distressed as they pulled the girl to her feet, and they all ran into the woods.

I was more confused now. Then, just as I started to wonder what was going on, a voice clearly said,

"Liam."

I froze, feeling a chill go down my spine. Then, as I turned to see who had called, I realized the sun was no longer shining. Instead, the moonlight reflected upon the still lake water, and crickets sang from the trees. I looked all around me but saw no one, and yet I heard a voice call my name again, this time closer.

"Who's there?" I asked, eyes searching for any signs of movement. I could hear my heart thundering away in my chest. No answer, just an eerie stillness. I shifted my feet in the sand, debating on making a run for it, when a hand grasped me around my ankle and dragged me down. I scraped my fingers against the sand, trying to claw my way out of the grasp of whoever or whatever had me, but I wasn't strong enough. My body slipped into the lake, deep under the surface. I spun around to see that my attacker was the girl I had dreamed of before. Her pale hands gripped at my chin, and her ghostly face came in close to mine as she screamed a stream of bubbles.

14

I screamed myself awake again, falling off of the motel bed and onto the shaggy brown carpet. I quickly got up and dusted myself off, sitting back down on the edge of my bed. Damian was already up, sitting at the small table, all sorts of photocopied documents and papers laid out in organized piles in front of him. He looked over at me, raising his eyebrows with concern.

"You OK?" he asked.

"Just another bad dream," I said, going over to the table. Damian pushed a coffee cup towards me, and I picked it up with no hesitation.

The smell of slightly burnt coffee stung at my nostrils, but I was still thankful for the caffeine. I pressed the styrofoam to my lips, drinking as much as I could before placing the cup upon the table, scrunching my nose, and smacking my lips with distaste.

"Where did you even get this?" I asked Damian, looking from the cup to him. "It tastes like mud."

My brother looked up from the papers he was poring over, struggling with his words as he found his thoughts.

"The uh, the...it's in the uh, the hall...the vending machine. I got it from the motel vending machine. You owe me seventy-five cents, by the way," he added, sitting more upright in his chair as he grabbed a pen from the table.

"What?" I asked, watching as Damian leaned over, circling words. The pen cap was still between his teeth as he spoke, his gaze still fixed on the paper.

"Look at this," Damian said as he rotated the page towards me, tapping his fingers against the fresh ink. "A girl was reported missing from Camp Hollyfalls in 1942. And then here—" he trailed off, flicking through other pages and slapping another photocopied article next to the one he had already indicated. He tapped the headline, "a boy in '54 drowned in the camp lake, and then here—" Damian pulled out a handful of other pages, all with the faces of children next to the byline. "'69, '73, '78, '82, '85, '94; Liam, it goes on like this! It's honestly insane that they kept this place open for so long."

"So, what are you thinking?" I asked slowly.

"I think there's a lot more that's going on here. Do you think you can help me out? I did a lot of research, but this is a two-person job."

"Yeah, sure. What do you want me to do?"

"Can you look up some of these names? There's like fifteen of 'em here, so if we split them up, it won't take as long."

"OK, yeah. Anything in particular I should be looking for?"

"Well, if any of them were ever found, for one. If any of these kids turned out happy and healthy, that's great - but if these kids all just vanished? I want to know why. If there were any connections, or what? Like, we went to Camp Hollyfalls, Liam. How come we were safe?"

"Our parents got eaten by ghosts or whatever, so we didn't exactly make it unscathed..."

"Dude, would you just focus on this? Here, go look up what you can on these kids," Damian said as he scrawled down a list of names. I took a moment, hovering over each name.

Eleanor Stodge, Jack Warner, Beth Deerling, Warren Fogerty, Kate Nelson, Sam Peters, and Greg Howell...

"Hey, didn't we go to camp with Greg Howell?"

I thought back to my days at camp, trying to put a name to a face. If I remembered correctly, Greg had been a tiny kid, shorter than all the other boys by about a head, and he always wore a pair of glasses with thick red frames. He was a nice enough kid, but I didn't remember him hanging out with anyone.

Damian went to work on investigating his list, and I did the same, going through what seemed like endless databases. I soon gathered a rough amount of information on most of the names I had been given, save for Eleanor Stodge. All I knew about her was that she was the first person reported missing from the camp. I searched for her on every database, and nothing came up, not even the Hollyfalls story.

"Hey, you got this name right, right? Cuz it seems like Eleanor Stodge doesn't exist." I said as I looked over at Damian, who nodded without even looking up.

"Yeah, her name is mentioned in a few of the articles."

"So, why can't I find her anywhere? Every search comes up with nothing. I get that she's from the forties, so I'm not expecting tons of info, but she has no trace, not even the news of her disappearance! It's like she never even existed."

Damian frowned and mouthed the name 'Eleanor Stodge' as he typed the name into the search field on his laptop, and after a few minutes, I heard a "huh" come from him.

"I definitely saw her name, though? Here lemme…"

"What are you doing?" I asked curiously.

"I'm gonna pull up the other articles and see if I can dredge up the name that way," Damian said as he hit ctrl+f and typed the name again.

"What?! That's so weird," Damian said, scratching his head. "She's really not coming up…but I know I saw the name."

"Maybe you imagined it."

"Yeah….yeah maybe. Anyway, I went through these other names to see if I could find a link anywhere, besides them all being campers, and guess what?"

"Go on."

"You're supposed to ask me 'what?'"

"Oh my god…"

"OK, whatever, the point is I found two things. One, all of the campers that were found dead or went missing were all staying in the same cabin, and two, the last place anyone saw these kids alive was by the lake."

I didn't know why, but I felt my skin crawl when Damian mentioned a lake.

"You think there's a connection?" I asked.

"I mean, probably. I don't know what yet, since the cabin they all stayed at was actually the farthest one from the lake, but I think it's a solid lead. Anyway, it's too late to go exploring a haunted camp with a high body count right now, so why don't we settle in for the night and head over first thing in the morning?"

"Yeah, OK. That sounds fine."

15

We spent the rest of our night unwinding. I ordered pizza from a local restaurant, and Damian ran down to a convenience store for sodas and chips. For those few hours that we sat on our beds, watching tv from our laptops and eating snacks, I felt normal.

I dreamed of her again that night, the girl in the lake. Her fear was my fear, and her scream was my scream. When I finally awoke, I was tired and cranky. I said nothing to my brother as we dressed and left the room, nor did I say anything as we drove towards the camp. I felt uneasy, like when you're nervous before a big test. My stomach was in knots, and there was this unseen weight pressing upon my chest and shoulders, and it only seemed to get heavier as we drew closer to the camp.

I unconsciously held my breath as the car turned off the paved road and onto a thin trail that led through the woods. I clenched my hands, my nails digging into the cushion of my seat with every bump of the road until finally, we crossed the threshold of Camp Hollyfalls. We were back.

The camp had, very obviously, not been well looked after. Weeds were growing all over the property in thick patches. The once canary yellow paint on the signs and roofs had become sun-bleached and chipped. The wooden structures themselves looked rotted and weak, as though they could collapse at any moment. And as we sat there in the car, looking at the camp, I realized that I could not hear birds chirping or crickets. It was dead silent.

We got out of the car, and Damian let out a low whistle as he came up upon one of the cabin sides, reaching out a hand to brush moss away, revealing the words "cabin five."

"The victims all stayed in cabin four, so that might be a good place to start, right?" he asked.

I nodded, craning my neck around to find the next building. "Over there," I said when I spotted a small dilapidated building. It was farther back, closer to the front entrance, and in a greater state of disrepair than the other structures. I stepped toward it, walking through the unkempt grass, and after a few paces, I heard the slight creak of rotted wood beneath my feet. Swiping my foot to the left, the words "cabin four" were just barely visible under caked-on grime.

"This is it," I said as Damian followed me towards the cabin. As we walked across the front porch, feeling the wooden planks sag beneath our weight, I felt my hesitation mount. Though it seemed silly and illogical, I felt like the cabin itself was *alive* and that we were disturbing it. I stopped short of the entryway, watching the splintered door swing slightly on its broken hinge to the rhythm of Damian's steps.

16

"**D**o you really think this is such a good idea?" I asked aloud, already knowing his answer.

"We've come this far, right?" Damian said, taking a flashlight out of his backpack and switching it on. "And we're getting paid to do this, so... we kinda gotta go through with this."

The light shone across the dirty floor, illuminating the small abandoned cabin. I spotted thick dust and leaves littering the floor, as well as some lost remnants of life. I could see a pair of socks someone had forgotten to pack, a bedspread bunched up on the floor with a large hole chewed out of it, and a few playing cards sticking out from between the floorboards. It just appeared to be a dirty old room, and I could see nothing particularly special or spooky about it.

"Should we go in or what, Sherlock?" Damian asked me, raising his eyebrows slightly, his expression a little judgmental.

"OK, fine," I said, and we both entered the cabin for a closer look. Once inside, I saw two bunk beds lining the room's walls. All of the beds had been stripped, leaving just stained mattresses rolled up in a corner and bare wooden frames pushed up against the wall. Now that I was properly in the room, I saw that it didn't look as though it had been packed up; it looked like it had been searched. But for what? On the far side of the cabin, papers and belongings were strewn all over the floor. I supposed it could have been an animal, but this didn't strike me as the work of a curious beast.

I stepped over a discarded baseball bat, trying not to tread on anything important when my heart froze in my chest. I could hear the pounding in my ears as my eyes saw the small, partly covered photograph caught beneath a dresser. Gulping, I bent down, lifting the furniture up enough to avoid ripping the photograph, and slid it out. As I turned the image to look at it, I let out a little yelp and dropped it, edging back.

"What is it?!" Damian called out, running over to my side, frantically shining his flashlight in every nook. "Did you see something?" Damian reached for the photograph I had dropped, lightly blowing the dust off its frayed edges. In the tiny photo sat a small girl, her dark hair hanging in perfect curls all about her face. It would have been a nice photograph had the eyes of the girl not been scratched out.

"The girl in that photo...I've been dreaming about her...she's been haunting me," I said, pointing at the disturbing photograph.

Damian turned the photo over in his hands, noting a handwritten scrawling at the bottom of the picture.

"Eleanor Stodge, 1942...Liam, this is it! This is her!" Damian exclaimed, handing the photo back. He was excited but dialed it back as he looked over at me. "Wait, you've been dreaming about her? Why didn't you tell me?"

I shrugged my shoulders. "I just thought it was a nightmare...I didn't want to trouble you." I said sheepishly, rubbing the back of my neck awkwardly, feeling the cold sweat that lingered there.

"Liam, you're the real deal. You are a *ghost whisperer.* If we didn't already have proof, this would be proof! So what happened in the dreams?"

I swallowed hard as I thought back on my nightmares, picturing her gaunt face, the lake...

"Well, in the first one, she was being chased, and then...and then pulled into the lake. And in the other one, I dunno, I was actually there, and I saw a bunch of people from a long time ago..."

"What do you mean?" Damian asked.

"Like...they were wearing old fashioned clothes. Not just like the forties, but also like, the sixties or seventies? I was always by the lake, and I couldn't quite hear what was going on, but each time I saw these people, they began panicking and then the girl, Eleanor, she called to me, she knew my name, and she pulled me under the water..." I ran my hand over my shoulder, rubbing the spot for support. Damian's mouth was slightly agape, and when he next spoke, his voice shook.

"Liam...do you think...do you think Eleanor is behind all of this?"

I didn't get a chance to answer as a loud SLAM came from behind us. We both jumped at the sound, turning around to see the door banging on its hinges.

"Just the wind?" Damian offered lamely. He got to his feet and craned his neck around the door before nodding

82

his head out, an unspoken 'let's get out of here.' I didn't need an excuse to want to leave; I got to my feet, dropping the photograph into Damian's open bag, and then followed him out into the midday sun.

"So what do we do now? If Eleanor is behind all of this, how do we stop her? There's no trace of her, no way to really find her. I know that you can destroy a ghost by burning their bones, but—"

"I don't think it's Eleanor," I interrupted, shoving my hands into my pockets as I stepped off the porch, heading down the graveled path.

17

"What are you talking about?! You said Eleanor was haunting you!" Damian said in exasperation.

"She is, but I don't think she's doing it to be malevolent. On the contrary, I think she's trying to tell me something. I think—" I trailed off, thinking about the moment in my dream in which she had tried to speak to me underwater. I tried to focus on the sound that escaped the stream of desperate bubbles, "—I think she was trying to ask me for help."

Damian took in a deep breath as he kept pace with me, obviously struggling with the information I had revealed.

"OK, so let's say that Eleanor is innocent, and she wants help...from what, Liam?"

"I don't know, but maybe taking a look at the lake might have some answers," I said with a shrug, trying to come off as braver than I felt.

Together, the two of us walked through the rest of the camp, looking at everything with scrutiny. We both were looking for signs that could point us in the right direction, anything that might give us a hint as to what we were dealing with. It did not take long for me to find the right path to the lake. As we walked through the woods, the sunlight filtering in through the leaves, I recognized where I was from my dreams. Finally, when the path stopped, we found ourselves upon the sandy bank, looking out at the black, murky water of the large man-made lake. When we were kids, I had been too scared to go out in the camp's kayaks and canoes. Knowing what I did now, I was glad I had never wanted to go out on the water.

We walked up the dock and to the edge, both of us looking hard at the one boat that was docked and still floating. I didn't want to get in that thing, but I could tell that Damian did. His eyes met mine, and there was an unspoken understanding.

"After you," I said, motioning with my hands for him to go first.

Damian cautiously clambered into the old rowboat and eased himself into the rear seat. I watched as he picked up the oars from the bottom of the boat and slid them into place before looking at me expectantly.

"Well? C'mon Cousteau! We've only got a few more hours until sundown, and I can't imagine this place will be less creepy in the dark."

That was for sure. I forced myself into the boat, taking the seat near the bow, gripping the sides tightly as Damian began to row. As we made our way across the lake, I watched our surroundings, looking for anything to help us. I couldn't stop thinking of all of those kids over the years, how this had been where they disappeared...

"Liam..."

18

"What?" I asked, only to be met with a look of confusion from my brother. Damian shook his head, "I didn't say anything."

"*Liam,*" the whisper was soft, barely audible over the lapping of the water. It was so discreet that I almost did not believe I had heard it, but then I heard it again.

"Stop! Stop rowing," I said to Damian, looking over the side of the boat and peering into the depths below as best I could. It was no easy feat as the lake had to be three miles long and two miles wide, meaning it was probably at least sixty feet in depth.

"What's up?" Damian asked, setting the oars down and maneuvering himself closer to where I was, his eyes trained on the water as well.

"I heard her. I heard Eleanor," I gasped, "I think she wants me to see something here." Though what, I could not say. We were well away from the shore, and the water was so dark that I could not see even an inch beneath its surface. So, what did she want me out here for? I pulled a face, grimacing, as I thought of the most viable solution to my problem.

"Nah, no, no WAY!" I said aloud, shaking my head and crossing my arms.

"Liam! What the hell?!" Damian asked loudly.

"I think she wants me to get in the water, and that's a huuuuuge nope!" I said, glancing from the water to my brother and back. There was no way I was getting into that water, and not just because the lake happened to be one of the sites of some very active haunting activity.

"You sure someone has to go in?" Damian asked, looking at the water as well.

I wasn't entirely sure; I had just made an educated guess. Why else would the ghost of a missing girl call for me while out here? I nodded solemnly.

He looked a little grim, but in a moment, Damian lifted his leg up, pulling his boots from his feet and placing them beneath his bench.

"Damian, wha —."

"I know you don't want to do this, so let me go," he said, stripping off his sock before going for his other foot. I tried to protest, to think of an alternative, but Damian simply shook his head as he stripped down.

"Liam, I'm your brother, and since mom and dad...," he trailed off, looking across at the water, before continuing solemnly, "It's my job to take care of you, so I'm doing this." He said, sitting on his bench in nothing but his boxer shorts and the silver prayer necklace that belonged to our mother. "I'll go in...just tell me what I'm looking for," Damian said resolutely.

The two of us stared at one another for a moment before I nodded and helped him into the water. He hissed with distaste immediately.

"It's freaking cold as frick!" he complained, treading water, "OK, I'm in, so what does ghost girl want us to find?"

I had no idea. I shrugged, which warranted a groan from Damian, who simply took in a deep breath and dove beneath the surface. As he disappeared beneath the water, I waited with bated breath, watching the spot where he had submerged.

"He needs to find it..."

I shuddered when I heard the voice, flinching as I noticed her leaning up against the side of the boat. Her skin was blue and waterlogged, her face was gaunt, and her hair was a tangle of dark mats and seaweed. She stared up at me with pupilless eyes, resting her chin upon the edge of the boat. My breathing quickened; I inhaled and exhaled sharply through my nose as I stared at her, plastered to my seat with fear. I was terrified of her, but Eleanor either did not notice, or she did not care. Then, her lips parted, and a soft whisper filled the air, *"He needs to find it..."*

"Find what?" I asked frantically. "What does he need to find?"

She reached out a hand to me, curling her forefinger in a beckoning way. I hesitated, trembling as I got closer to her. "What does he have to search for?" I asked again.

Just as she was beginning to speak, someone yelled from shore.

"JUST WHAT DO YOU THINK YOU'RE DOING?!"

19

I snapped my attention to the shore to see an older man in coveralls at the docks, his face red from exertion. "GET OUT OF THAT LAKE RIGHT NOW!"

It took a moment for me to register what had happened. I blinked slowly and looked around; the ghost of Eleanor had disappeared, but Damian had resurfaced, hoisting his wet body back into the boat. The two of us rowed back to shore and were immediately intercepted by the ornery older man. As our boat reached the dock, the old man grabbed me by the front of my shirt and pulled me away from the water. He was surprisingly strong, despite appearances.

"What were you idiots doing out there?!" he yelled, grabbing Damian by his arm and pushing us both into the sand. "I should have you both arrested for trespassing! This is private property!"

"We have permission from the owners," Damian said, and I didn't know for sure if that was true.

"Why in the heck would they give you dinguses permission to be here, let alone out on that lake?" The old man demanded gruffly. Clearly, he had decided that there was no longer a use for him to be cordial or polite in his advanced age. He was easily one of the rudest men that I had ever met in my life, and that was saying something.

"We're investigators, and we're looking into the deaths and disappearances of several campers."

"What in the hell would they need to hire investigators for?! Kids died, and the camp was permanently shut down. What good is dredging up the past?!"

The way that the old man spoke made me feel suspicious. I gave a sideways glance to Damian, who gave a knowing face in response.

"Well, depending on what we find, they could potentially open the place up again."

"You are wasting your time! Look, I'm the caretaker for this place. I would love to see this place up and running again, believe you me, but that ain't never gonna happen! Do you hear me? Now clear off!" The man's lower lip jutted out as his jaw clenched, his face stern as he pointed a finger back towards the main gate.

"You can't tell us to leave!" Damian sputtered out.

"Just did! Now get!" the old man said through clenched teeth.

Damian opened his mouth to protest, but I nudged him in the ribs. "No, we can go. We'll just call up the family and let them know there was some resistance...one of their employees wasn't letting us do our job." Damian quickly understood what I was trying to do. He let out a dramatic sigh and kicked at the sandy ground, "They'll be frustrated. They told me they didn't want us to take too long and that they would make sure we had every resource."

I looked to the old man to see if any cogs were going around in his head, but to my dismay, he didn't seem afraid of us running to his bosses.

"They've had plenty of disappointments in the past! You call em' up, and you tell them that Ed said to let the past stay buried!"

We relented with frowns upon our faces, allowing old Ed to shepherd us back to the car. The old man had eagle eyes, watching us like a bird of prey as we left, keeping his eye on us until the car had gone up the dirt road and out of his sight.

Damian let out a frustrated yell when we reached the highway, thumping his fist upon the dashboard several times.

"That stupid old geezer! We almost had something, and then he just ruins everything!" Damian lamented. He then looked over at me and made another frustrated sound.

"Liam, what the hell? Why aren't you upset too?!"

"Because," I said calmly, turning my head towards my window and pressing my forehead against the cool glass, "We can just go back later. It's not like he can watch the grounds all day and night."

A smile broke across Damian's face as he looked at me, nodding his head encouragingly, "Look at you! OK, let's grab some dinner, go back to the motel, and just wait it out, then come back and see if we can find what's in that lake." Damian said with conviction. I nodded along with the plan, a little hesitant about going back to the lake but agreeing with what we needed to do. There was clearly something in that lake that we needed to uncover. The way that the ghost had spoken and how she said 'he needs to bring it up' made me think that it was crucial. Part of me thought it would be her lost body, but I didn't want to entertain that thought.

20

The next few hours seemed to drag on forever, and I kept looking at the clock, waiting for what seemed like the right time. Dinner was over too fast, and then we were back at the motel, watching cable tv and drinking sodas. Well, I was – Damian was fixated upon his laptop, trying to investigate further. His brow was furrowed, and he did not seem to realize he had taken to chewing on the end of his pen.

"Something good?" I asked absently, turning my attention back to the television. Damian hummed thoughtfully before responding.

"Well...I think so," Damian said, turning his screen towards me. "I think I found Eleanor."

I took the laptop from Damian and began to read, stopping shy of the first sentence. "Damian, this is just a list of local legends," I said.

"OK, yeah, but read it," Damian assured me.

I sighed and then began to read aloud.

"It is said that the ghost of a young girl haunts Lake Hollyfalls. In 1942, Eleanor went swimming in Lake

Hollyfalls with her younger brother Edward. Despite their parents' warnings about an incoming storm, the two continued to swim and were caught in a horrible downpour. The children struggled to swim to safety but were swallowed by the waves. When the storm passed, only Edward was recovered alive. Unfortunately, Eleanor's body was never found. Since her death, over fifteen children have died at her hands."

As I finished reading, I turned my gaze to Damian, who looked mildly concerned. "So, what do you think?" Damian asked.

I felt a weird pit in my stomach, but I tried to reason with it a bit. "Damian, this is written on a blog called *'Talk Ghostie To Me,'* do you really think this is the most reliable source?" I asked, only to be met with an eye-roll from Damian.

"You do realize we're on a ghost hunt, right? That we've already encountered the ghost in the lake, and it all makes sense? Dude, it's Eleanor! Eleanor is the one behind everything!"

I didn't know what to think. "But she...she was helping. In the dream, she was the one being chased. Something was after her. It doesn't make sense."

Damian shook his head. "What if she was just making that up? I mean, she was manipulating your dreams. What if that was just to lure us here?"

"Why, though? Why lure me? The story says that the ghost goes after children, and we aren't kids. So why would she go after us?"

"Well, the camp is shut down now, right? She doesn't have access to new kids, so she would need the camp to be reopened. So she used you." Damian said matter of factly.

"We can't get the camp reopened if she's the one killing kids!" I reasoned.

"Look, I don't know, man. If she was smart enough to lure you here, maybe she's also smart enough to pin all these deaths on someone else. Of course, she's a ghost, and I don't know what motive she's supposed to have."

"That's definitely what I would want to know. Why? Why would she want to do any of this?" I asked.

This was the million-dollar question, and I had no answer. It wasn't like Damian and I had much experience with this. We had only been on one ghost hunt before, and I wasn't even altogether sure we had encountered a real ghost. Damian and I may have thought those things that ate our parents were ghosts originally, but after everything we've learned since, I'm not so sure.

"Well, she drowned in a terrible storm, didn't she? I'm pretty sure this is the sort of traumatic crap that may have you wanting to hurt people," Damian said, his voice edging on exasperation.

I shook my head, though I couldn't help but feel a little swayed.

"Look, I've been reading up on it, and this sounds like a vengeful spirit. Whatever the plan was before, it has changed. We have to stop Eleanor," Damian said, shutting the laptop and scooting off the bed, heading towards the side table and grabbing a bag of chips.

"OK, so, let's say that's the plan. We have to stop Eleanor, but how?" I asked.

"Salt and burn the bones," Damian said with a loud CRUNCH as he shoved a handful of chips in his mouth. "Like last time."

"How does that help? We don't even know where her bones are." I said impatiently.

"Remember, what I've been reading says that salt acts as a purifying agent. It absorbs negative energy. Lots of biblical mumbo jumbo, but the fact is that salt makes it so the flames can conduct a cleansing burn of the bad spirit." Damian said succinctly.

"But we have no way of doing that without the bones! Besides this story, there is no trace of Eleanor Stodge. For all intents and purposes, she doesn't exist. There's no way to find her body." I said.

"The lake," Damian said in all but a whisper. "Her body is in the lake,"

I shook my head. "They never found her body, Damian. So what, you think we're going to be able to do what the police couldn't?"

"Liam, the police in the forties barely knew how to find fingerprints. You actually think they were competent enough to dredge a lake?" Damian said, considerable amounts of sass in his voice. "We can find her, put her to rest, put a stop to this."

I shook my head again, but he was winning me over. Even if Eleanor wasn't the true reason behind all the missing persons and deaths, she still deserved to be put to rest. In fact, the more I thought about it, the more I felt that maybe that was the reason she had reached out to me. We could finally uncover her body and give Eleanor peace.

21

"OK, so that's the plan," I said calmly, taking a swig of soda and looking at the clock once more. 2:00 a.m.

"I think it's about time we head out," I said, nodding towards the door. Damian agreed, and we packed up our things and headed out to the car. This car ride was quick, and before I knew it, the car had come to a halt outside the camp. Damian and I quickly got out, grabbed our bags, and began hiking down the trail towards the lake. With flashlights in hand, we kept our steps lit, watching our progression, as well as for any other signs of movement. We may have been up here on a ghost expedition, but we did not want to anger a Copperhead, or a Black Widow, or whatever creepy crawlies might have been lurking in the shadows.

As we walked down the path, my mind began racing, thinking over everything we had discussed over the last forty-eight hours. My thoughts mainly swirled around things concerning Eleanor. I just couldn't wrap my head around all of it. Could she be the baddie in this nightmare?

Why would she kill all these children? Moreover, why did she reach out to me in the first place? That question stuck with me for a while as I remembered the first night I had dreamed of her. She looked scared, like there was something else to fear.

My feet crunched across the gravel path that led into the cool sand of the lakeshore. I remembered this place, the way it looked, from my dream. The moonlight shimmered across the dark water, providing us with enough light to see. Damian and I both looked around, taking in the scenery, and again I noticed absolute silence. No owls hooting or crickets chirping; there was nothing to be heard outside of our own breathing. I felt my heartbeat in my throat as I saw the boat at the dock, knowing that the two of us would once again have to row out into the lake.

"You ready for this?" Damian asked me, and I could hear the slight hesitation in his voice. For the first time in a long time, Damian genuinely seemed apprehensive, maybe even scared. Of course, I shared the feeling, but I clapped my brother on the back, nodding all the while.

"I'm as ready as I'll ever be. Are you?" I asked in response, doing my best to put on a brave face.

Damian pulled on a matching grin and nodded at me, even managing a short chuckle. "Yeah, let's do this! In, out, get paid! Piece of cake," Damian said aloud, which I was pretty sure was to psych himself up. I was doing the same in my own way, telling myself that Eleanor needed to be put to rest. It was the right thing to do.

We tossed our duffels into the boat and again clambered in. I grabbed the oars and began to paddle, watching the blades disturb the water in large ripples. So far, so good; nothing scary had come out yet to spook us, to harm us. Finally, we made it to the middle of the lake, and this was the part that was going to be the most difficult. When I placed the oars down at the bottom of the boat, Damian and I exchanged a look. Now for the hard part – finding the body.

We both began to undress until we were sitting in our swim trunks; we had come prepared this time. Then, headlamps fastened in place, the both of us carefully tipped over the side of the boat, landing into the cold water. I yelped with shock, which was met by a choppy laugh on Damian's part.

"S-s-s-see?" he asked, shivering as he spoke, "it's fr-fr-fr-fr-freaking c-c-cold!"

I groaned as I flailed my arms and legs about, trying to adjust as quickly as possible to the frigid water. Once I had, I pushed the button on my waterproof headlamp, and the light sprang into life.

"OK, let's give this a shot!" I said breathily, the chill still in my chest. Damian nodded in agreement, and we counted off.

ONE...

TWO...

THREE!

On three, we both dove beneath the surface, swimming off in different directions to cover more ground. I kicked my feet hard to get as close as I could to the bottom, shining my light along the lake floor, searching for something that might connect me to Eleanor. The trouble was, I could not see anything distinct hiding at the bottom...or anything indistinct. I just saw more darkness, a din which our cheap light sources could not break through. It was just too far down. The lake was too deep;

there was no way I would be able to swim to the bottom without SCUBA gear. It was impossible.

I chose to resurface, kicking my legs hard until my head broke through the surface. I gasped for air as I shot out, flailing around as I realized that only I had come up.

22

"Damian?" I called out, whipping my head in all directions. "Damian?" I called again, a little more urgency in my voice.

A moment later and Damian broke the surface a few feet away from me, gasping like a fish out of water.

"You jerk, I was starting to get worried!" I shouted over at him.

Damian only continued to gasp for air. "It's not my fault I can hold my breath longer than you!" he finally said as he bobbed around in the water. "Did you find anything?" he asked.

"No," I said in a somewhat defeated voice, "It's too deep. We'll never be able to get anything from down there. This was a bad plan." I said, swimming closer to Damian. "Let's go back to the boat. Come up with a plan B."

Damian agreed, and we headed back, helping each other clamber back in. My belly slid over the wooden side, and I overshot my mark, my body catching the bench in my ribs, making me groan as I fell to the floor of the boat.

"Wow, such grace," Damian jested as he helped me up.

"Shut up," I said as I sat back down on my bench. This time Damian took the oars and paddled us back to shore. It was better this way, as I started to feel pretty defeated. There was no way we were going to be able to find her body, not without a proper crew to dredge the lake, and the chances of us being able to convince even one person to come out and look for a body? Well...honestly, that part maybe; there were a lot of people who might come out for the thrill of it, but not the kind of people that I would want with us; no one would help that would be beneficial.

I was starting to give up hope, to feel like a failure, when I saw something glinting on the opposite shore. It looked like a string of silver caught on a log.

"Damian! Look at that!" I shouted, pointing in the new direction. Damian quickly turned the bow to the left and carried us quickly to the alternate shore. As we drew closer, I could see it more clearly. It looked like a silver necklace caught in the felled branches. I reached out my arm as we came in close, stretching out my fingers to the fullest extent.

"Just a little closer!" I said with urgency, extending myself slightly over the edge as the pads of my fingers gently brushed against the tarnished silver. I could feel the chain across my palm, and I closed my fingers upon it, pulling firmly to free it from its snarled prison. I feared for a moment that I would break it, that the force from my pull would make the chain snap.

"Ugh, I think it's stuck! Just give me a sec—"

I felt something strong and cold grab me around my middle and tug me down. I heard Damian scream out my name as I hit the water, flailing around, grabbing at the log, and holding on for dear life. Whatever had me began to pull harder, trying to pull me down.

"Liam! Liam! Grab hold!" Damian yelped as he flung himself to the side of the boat, reaching out for me. I tried to turn around, to see the thing that had me, but the water was too dark.

I pulled myself tightly to the log, hugging it close to my body. The branches and brambles scratched at my face, cutting my face and my arms, but I would not let go. I couldn't, or I'd disappear beneath the depths.

The grip on me strengthened, and the dragging became more erratic. It felt like an alligator had taken me by the legs and was trying to roll me under. The trouble was that while it got stronger, I was starting to get sore and exhausted. I didn't want to let go because letting go would be the end...but I could only last for so long.

"Damian! You need to get out of here!" I shouted, trying to get a tighter grip.

"Liam, no! Shut up! I'm not leaving without you—"

"Listen," I shouted, "you need to go! You have to get out of here! I can't hold on for much longer! Get out before it gets you!"

Damian cursed but didn't leave. Instead, he dug through the duffel and pulled out one of the containers of salt we had bought on the way back to Hollyfalls. Damian poured a handful into his hand and then threw it over the side, making the creature bellow and briefly release me from its clutches. I scrambled forward, trying to get closer to shore, but feeling the freezing hands wrap once more around my ankles. I screamed in pain as I was pulled roughly, doing my best to keep my head above water but barely able to do so. My face was all but submerged as I struggled to keep my mouth above the surface, but I couldn't.

I felt myself being dragged down. I could hear Damian's muffled yell, but it was over. I was going to die.

Or so I thought. I saw a projectile speed towards me, hitting the thing that had me, making it scream in agony. I kicked away as fast as I could, scrambling to the surface. As I broke into the night air, I sucked in as much oxygen as I could, coughing up water as I moved toward the water's edge. I struggled because of my exhaustion, but I soon found strong arms picking me up and helping me to the shore.

"Thanks, Damian, I—"

"I told you idiots not to come here, didn't I?!?"

23

I looked to my side to see the angered face of Ed, the caretaker, by my side. His face was blanched, white as a sheet with worry, but his voice was still gruff.

"I-I uh," I sputtered as I struggled to my feet, hearing frantic splashing as Damian ran over to us, pulling me into a quick hug.

"Liam! God, I thought you—" Damian said, his voice choked up.

"If you two morons could finish up the feelings fest, we still have a poltergeist to deal with," Ed said, cocking a gun and pointing it back at the lake.

"Jesus, Ed!" Damian said, eyeing up the gun. Ed just looked over at him as though understanding the unasked question hanging in the air.

"The bullets are made from pure iron. Hurts ghosts pretty good. Been using it to keep this one in check," he said, looking through the viewfinder.

"What the hell?! You know about the ghost?!" I shouted.

"Of course, I know about her! I told you idiots to stay away for a reason! Now come on, back up to the cabins. She doesn't like to go far from the lake, so we might be able to buy some time up there."

Ed pushed Damian and me up the path, though we didn't need to be told twice. The three of us kept a quick pace as we headed back up to the camp. Ed constantly threw a look over his shoulder, ensuring that there was nothing following.

"You seem to know a lot about this ghost, Ed," I said, needling him for info.

"I've made it my business to know her. She's my problem." He said brusquely.

"Why? Did you kill her?"

The question had barely left my lips when I felt my body lifted off the ground and pressed roughly against the trunk of a tree. Ed had me pinned, his hand around my throat.

"I never hurt her," Ed said through gritted teeth, tears brimming at the corners of his eyes. "Eleanor was a good person. She cared about me like no one ever would. She was my best friend."

"Wait, you're Edward...aren't you," I asked, gulping as his grip only seemed to get tighter. "You're her brother."

Ed then let me go, heading back up the path.

"Ed! You were there when Eleanor died!" I called after him, quick on his heels.

"So?! A lot of people were there!" Ed growled.

"So, you know what really happened!" I persisted.

"You need to tell us what happened, Ed!" Damian exclaimed loudly as we both followed behind Ed.

"It was a long time ago!" Ed said, continuing to avoid answering our question. I was not going to give up, though, and I could tell that Damian would not either. So we continued to pester him like rowdy children until finally, Ed had reached his breaking point.

"I don't know what happened, OK!? I was a little boy! One minute we were swimming and having fun, and the next minute we were fighting for our lives!" Ed paused, taking in several breaths, before continuing. "The waves got too strong, and we couldn't tread water any longer...and Eleanor, she saved me. She held me up so I could hold onto a floatation device and...and after that, I never saw her alive again."

"She saved you? But— but why is she trying to kill people? Why is she doing this if she was the kind of person that would put your life before her own?" I asked.

"She was only eight when she died. So she's been a lonely kid for over almost a century. She doesn't want to be alone."

As Ed spoke, I realized what had been happening. Eleanor was taking children, not for vengeance against what had happened to her, but so she could have a friend forever.

"But, she wouldn't need to kill if that were true. Wouldn't she have dozens of ghost kid friends by now? Where are all those kids?" Damian asked.

Damian made a valid point, and I pondered this as we continued up towards the cabins. But, then, it hit me.

"The kids' bodies don't stay here. Instead, their parents bring them home for burials." That made sense to me.

"What about the missing kids?" Damian countered, and I had to admit, maybe he had me there. Unless maybe those kids that went missing had nothing to do with Eleanor.

"What if those kids aren't dead? Maybe they just went missing in like, a non-supernatural way?" I asked.

Damian opened his mouth to respond, but only a scream came out as he was dragged into the woods and off the trail.

24

"HEY!" I shouted, running after my brother and his captor. Ed followed quickly behind, firing off his shotgun in the direction they had headed in.

"Dude, be careful! You might shoot my brother!" I shouted as we ran, attempting to catch up with Damian and the ghost. I dove for Damian's hand, reaching for his wrist and tugging back. It was no use, though. I lost my grip and watched as Damian hurtled towards the water.

"NO!" I screamed, throwing myself at them one more time. My fingers clasped around Damian's wrist, and I anchored my legs around a log.

"Damian, don't let go!" I shouted.

"Liam, I don't think I can hold on for very long!" Damian yelled, his face screwed up in pain as the ghost tightened its grip.

"*He is mine,*" The ghosts' voice hissed over the noise of the struggle.

"NO, HE'S NOT!" I bellowed back, tugging hard, though losing my footing. We were slowly being dragged back into the lake. Damian was into the water up to his thighs. In all the struggle and energy spent, somewhere along the lines, Eleanor became visible. Her tiny body was contorted, black mats of hair covered her gaunt face.

"Noooo!" I yelled again, feeling the water creep up my calves as we were dragged further into the lake. It was futile, but I was not going to give up. I had already lost my parents, and I wasn't going to lose my brother too.

"Damian, don't let go!" I whimpered, pulling back, gaining a few inches but soon losing what I had gained.

"Liam, it's too late! Just let go!" Damian cried, tears stinging at the corners of his eyes as his grip slackened in my hand.

"No, Damian! You didn't leave me earlier, so I'm not going to abandon you! Don't give up, Damian! Please!" I cried out, tears filling my eyes and blurring my vision.

"ELEANOR, STOP!" Ed shouted, standing just beyond the water.

The grip on Damian loosened, sending both of us back to shore as I tugged. Eleanor stood in the water, her hair limp around her face, staring at Ed with her milky white eyes.

"You need to stop this, Eleanor! You need to stop taking people!" Ed shouted, his chin quivering slightly but his voice strong. "Let them go. Let them leave this place," Ed said, his stance becoming stronger. Eleanor tilted her head, letting the dark clumps of her hair fall away, revealing her skeletal body.

"I need them. I don't want to be alone anymore," Eleanor's voice was raspy. As she stood before us, thunder rolled in, and lightning flashed across the sky above us. She looked

sinister as she stood there; her decaying body reached out towards Damian and me.

"Ellie, you don't have to be alone anymore. You won't be alone anymore," Ed said, taking a few steps forward, standing up to his waist in the dark water. "I'll come with you."

Eleanor dropped her gaze from Damian and me, turning her entire focus onto Ed. Eleanor drew closer to Ed, getting within an inch of his face. *"You would do that...for me?"* Eleanor gurgled, her rotting jaw slackening with each word. She was a true horror, but Ed did not falter. Instead, the old man stared straight into the ghost's cloudy eyes, his demeanor strong.

Ed nodded, holding out his arms to embrace her. The ghost looked confused at first, regarding his arms as a mouse would a trap, but then she came around. She came forward, reaching her arms around Ed.

"Come play with me, little brother," Eleanor whispered before pulling Ed beneath the surface of the water.

"Ed, no!" I shouted, jumping forward but being caught around the middle by Damian. "Liam, no! Let him go! He made his choice!" Damian yelled, pulling me back.

"No, we can still save him! We can end this! Just let me—Damian! Let me go!" I shouted, struggling against his grip but giving up in a heap, crying. Damian gave me a quick hug before pulling me to my feet.

"Liam, we have to go! Let's go!" Damian said. I very reluctantly got to my feet, and as I did so, I heard the sound of laughter echoing from across the lake. I looked across the water and saw the phantasmal images of two small children splashing and playing before disappearing into the night.

25

"**A**lright, let's go," I said, watching as Damian turned around, and we both sprinted up the path and to our car. I don't even remember the car ride back to the motel or how I found myself clean and dry and in my pajamas. Everything seemed like it was moving on fast-forward, and all I had left to do was dream. I stretched out across my bed, trying to get comfortable, but my thoughts would not rest. Something just was not sitting right with me, and I did not know what it was.

I tossed and turned, rolling from side to side on my mattress, listening to the coiled springs creak as I kept repositioning myself. Then, after what felt like an hour of this unsettled restlessness, Damian finally lost his temper with me.

"Christ, Liam. What is the damn problem?" he asked, his voice grumpy as he threw off his covers and sat up in bed. Hoisting his legs over the side, Damian turned to look at me.

"We figured out what was going on at Camp Hollyfalls, and we stopped a ghost from taking any more lives. We did a good thing here!" he explained in exasperation. I heard what he said, and I did not disagree, but it just seemed hollow.

"We didn't save Ed, though. We failed at keeping people safe," I said quietly, staring up at the ceiling.

"Liam, we're never going to be able to save everyone. That's just how life goes. Not everyone can be saved, but we can save a hell of a lot of people," Damian said, running his hands over his scalp.

I shook my head, "We haven't saved anyone... it's just a pile of corpses at our feet," I muttered under my breath.

"We have saved a lot of people, you dummy!" Damian said, clearly frustrated now.

"We couldn't save Ed, or Mom and Dad. We didn't sa—"

"Liam, shut up! Look, what happened to mom and dad was probably awful, but we couldn't have done anything to save them! We were just kids! Your balls hadn't even dropped yet. Do you really think that you and I could have stopped those cannibals? No! If we had been there, you and I would be dead too! We lived—"

"I wish we hadn't some times," I said thickly, tears sprouting from the corners of my eyes, first from my emotions and then from pain, as Damian walloped me hard in the shoulder. I yelled from the punch, only for Damian to curse at me again.

"For someone so smart, you really are dumb! Do you honestly think if mom and dad were alive that they'd want to hear you saying dumb stuff like that? No. You know damn well that they would want for us to keep going. Hell, I think they'd be proud of us for starting this business. We help people, no matter how badly you want to ignore that.

We helped Eleanor, didn't we? Maybe we couldn't find her body and put her to rest, but we reunited her with her brother. We stopped her from harming any more people. We saved hundreds of people, even if we never met them. What we do is much bigger than us, don't you see that?"

I could feel Damian's eyes on me, and so I shifted again, turning my back to him as I pretended to fall asleep. Damian said nothing else to me. I just heard him climb back under the covers and the flick of his bedside table lamp go out.

26

I forced my eyes shut and focused upon my breathing, counting each second between inhaling and exhaling until I finally fell asleep. As I drifted off, my body felt weightless and fuzzy, like I had had one too many drinks. It felt wrong, and as the feeling started to make me numb, I opened my eyes to find myself in an unfamiliar room. I got to my feet and walked across the room, listening to the sound of my heels clacking across the hardwood floors. As I stood by the window, I noticed my reflection and saw that I was not myself but in a well-dressed woman's body. The face that peered back at me was severe, with high cheekbones and brown hair pulled into such a tight bun that the skin across the forehead was tight. There were wrinkles around my eyes and mouth, and displeasure deepened the lines. Without my control, my body began to walk from the room, turning a corner and heading out of the house. My hands hoisted up the hem of my skirt as I walked down the stone steps to greet a man who was approaching.

"Oh, Martin! What dreadful news," the voice that came from my lips was sickeningly sweet, very high and breathy, much different than what I would have expected. "Eleanor was such a sweet little girl! I was growing quite fond of her."

The man called Martin embraced the woman briefly before beckoning for another to come up from the steps. A small boy with dark hair came up the steps, holding a teddy bear while tears streamed down his face.

"Oh, Edward! You come here, my little man!" I said, and I threw my arms open as I knelt to embrace the boy, but he ran past me into the house.

"The boy just lost his sister, and he lost his mother last winter. It may take him time to accept you as his new mother, Johanna." Martin said as he took me by the waist, leading me back into the house. I could feel myself pout, but somehow I knew that my heart was not in it, or Johanna's heart, that is.

Martin led me back into the house and brought me back to my chambers, giving me a peck on the cheek before telling me that we would have an early supper. When he closed the door, I went to my vanity, sitting upon the stool and staring into my reflection. My hands lifted, fluffing up my cheeks to bring out the rosy color in them before I began to speak.

"He doesn't see me as his mother, but he will see me as the mistress of this house," the words slipped from my lips with ease. Then, my fingers reached into the jewelry box across from me, withdrawing a beautiful silver locket. My vulture-like fingers dug at the clasp, prying the locket open and gazing at the photographs momentarily. Inside was a picture of Eleanor on one side and Edward on the other. My fingers ripped both photographs out and placed them upon the vanity table. I then withdrew a bobby pin, scratching it hard over the face of Eleanor, scratching until her eyes were gone.

"Only one child left to stand in my way," I said, holding up the photo of Edward. "It's a real shame...that storm was meant for both of you. I don't know how you managed to survive it, but you won't manage through the next one. That much, I promise, *darling.*"

I then began to laugh, a high, cruel laugh.

And then I awoke in a cold sweat, rolling out of bed and shaking Damian awake.

27

"What? What? Whaaat?" Damian whined as he rolled over, covering his head with his pillow as he tried to drown me out. That wasn't going to happen though; I would never allow it.

"Damian, wake up! We're not done! There really was something that pulled Eleanor down!" I said, continuing to shake my brother and trying to snatch the pillow from his grip.

"Ugh, what?" Damian said, letting me take the pillow as he sat up in his bed, blinking at me slowly, his gaze bleary-eyed as he ran his palms over his eyes to rub out the sleep.

"I just had another dream about Eleanor. This time I was in the body of her stepmother, seeing the world from her perspective. Dude, I think she might have been a witch, and she created that storm that killed Eleanor," I said as I took a seat at the end of Damian's bed. My face was white with shock as I said the words aloud, barely able to believe them myself.

Damian continued to blink slowly, absorbing my words, slowly comprehending them.

"Wait, so, so let me get this right. You think that Eleanor was—."

"Was murdered by her stepmother, yeah I do. The stepmom, Johanna, seemed like a cruel witch masquerading as a sweet woman. From what I saw, Eleanor and Ed's father wasn't very domineering, I guess? He seemed like the type of guy that would be easy for a woman like her to control," I continued, thinking about what I had seen, recalling the man's features. Mr. Stodge had been a slight man, barely over the height of five foot five inches. His skin was pasty, and he had a thin patch of dark brown hair plastered to his small head and a sparse handlebar mustache. He looked sickly, now that I thought about it.

"I think... OK, I think their father, Martin, was ill. He was sick, his wife had already died, and he was a widower with two young children," I stopped, thinking. I recalled the house I had been in, remembered the estate, the sprawling lawn I had seen from the window, and said, "He was a rich widower. This Johanna woman saw him as a prime target. She got in there, maybe charming him with magic, married him, and became a rich woman, but that wasn't enough for her. She knew he was dying, or she was making sure he was dying...which meant that...well, wouldn't she inherit everything? So why try and kill the children?"

Damian got up from his bed, heading for his laptop. He quickly opened a browser and began typing, speaking aloud as he did so. "Martin Stodge," he said as he clicked away at the keys, then brought his face closer to the screen as he scanned through the results, finally choosing a suitable link.

He read silently for a few minutes before finding something to share with me. "I've got it. So, it looks like the majority of Martin's wealth was actually his late wife's estate. He was a benefactor, but this says that if he were to predecease his children, the entire estate would be inherited by his son, Edward. There is no mention of Eleanor, but I mean…this checks out. And look, there's a picture of the family." Damian said, spinning the screen around so I could see the portrait.

Martin was standing there with his arm wrapped around the waist of a petit blond woman with a kind face. Eleanor was standing in front of the couple, with her hands reaching for her mother, but they were not the only people in the portrait. Another woman was also in the portrait, a tall severe-looking woman with dark ringlets all about her face.

"Damian, that's Johanna!" I said, pointing at the cruel-looking woman. Damian turned the screen back towards him to look at the photograph and to read the caption. "'Nanny, Johanna Highstaff, holds Edward Stodge,' Liam, she was their nanny! She was there with the first wife too! Oh my god, she probably killed the mom too! She murdered them…she murdered all of them!"

I looked at him resolutely and asked, "What happened to her? What happened to Johanna?"

Damian quickly searched for her name, which brought up a notice of a private burial in the family cemetery.

"So, she died?" I asked.

"It says here that the family estate burned down in 1944, with Johanna inside. She was buried in the family plot on the estate." Damian said, reading slowly.

"I guess it might take some time to find that if it doesn't say where their family estate was," I said, exasperated. I just wanted all of this to end.

"The house was not rebuilt, and instead, the grounds were turned into a camp for children, named for Mr. Stodge's late wife, Holly, whose family name was Fallon. Camp Hollyfalls will open for campers for the first time this spring...paper dated 1946." Damian's eyes were wide as he stopped reading, looking up at me with his mouth agape. "Liam, she's buried in the camp somewhere! She's buried at camp Hollyfalls!"

I was starting to feel overwhelmed. My heart was pumping hard in my chest as I tried to get my ideas straight, grasping at everything I had just learned. It was a complex task understanding a witch that had attempted to murder an entire family, as I had no idea up to this point that witches existed. However, as I had finally come to terms with the existence of ghosts, I was able to get around that. Witches existed, and one was the reason behind all of the tragedy at Camp Hollyfalls...and might still be able to harm.

"Damian, you know what we have to do, right?" I asked as I stood up, bending over to pick up my jeans from the bedroom floor and pull them on.

"Dude, right now? Why can't we just sleep first and take care of it in the morning?" Damian asked, whining.

"Because this is important! We have to get rid of this murderous witch, I can feel it. We have to set Eleanor, and now Edward, free and make sure Johanna never comes back. Plus—" and I picked up the digital clock from the bedside table, showing him the face, "It's five. Already morning time, bro." I said, setting the clock down and walking over to the door. I slipped my shoes on with ease, feeling the unpleasant sensation of wetness as my feet slid inside. A minor inconvenience, walking around in wet shoes, but I had bigger things to take care of.

Damian began to dress too, and in minutes we were back on the road, driving right back to Camp Hollyfalls, parking inside the main gate. It was not as dark anymore as the day would break soon, so I hoped it would not be too difficult to find the grave we were searching for.

28

"**O**K, where is it again?" I asked Damian, popping open the trunk and withdrawing a spade and my duffel bag. I unzipped the bag quickly, double checking that we had enough supplies. I packed three large canisters of salt, a can of lighter fluid, a box of matches, the gun with the iron bullets that had belonged to Ed, a bell, and a bunch of white sage wrapped in twine.

"You gonna read my tea leaves later, too?" Damian asked sarcastically at the sight of the sage. I just shrugged.

"I dunno. I have a feeling we're going to need it for this one. Just shut up, and let's go." I said, zipping the bag back up and shouldering it.

"From what I understand, the old family plot is actually near the lake. I think it's actually on the bank where you nearly got pulled under." Damian said as he took the spade from me, slinging it over his shoulder and beginning to walk.

"Luckily, we don't have to get in the boat this time. Pretty sure we can reach the graveyard if we trek this way," he said, leading me down a path that wasn't really a path at all. We cut through the trees and the brush, pushing branches aside as we stomped through the woods, moving quickly until I saw it.

"There!" I said, pointing my finger at a massive hunk of stone. We quickened our pace and soon found ourselves standing at the foot of the large stone bust of an angel. Thick moss covered the stone, obscuring the features and the decorated headstone. I stretched out a hand and began scratching away the muck and grime, making out the name that had been carved long ago. Damian began to help, and after several busy minutes, we had done it.

I stood back, clapping the moss and dirt from my hands as I read,

Here Lies Johanna Stodge
Beloved Wife and Mother

"Welp, here she is," Damian said, letting the head of his spade rest upon the earth. "Well, let's hurry up and do something before someone shows up."

"Dude, whose gonna show up? Ed was the caretaker, and I kinda doubt he's gonna stop us now," I said, dropping the duffle bag to the ground and rummaging around.

"Fair point," Damian said before he did the sign of the cross out of respect for the old man. "I'm letting you take the lead on this one. I feel like you know what to do."

I didn't, but I had a hunch about how to get rid of this evil spirit. So I handed Damian a canister of salt and directed him to sprinkle a thick line around the grave.

"This step is key. We need the salt to absorb the negative energy here," I said as I lit the sage and thick smoke filled the air.

I began to walk clockwise around the grave, wafting the smoke in the air. Then, after three slow circles, I spoke. "By the power of our good intentions, I ask the powers that be to remove negative entities from this space. You are no longer welcome here."

I held my breath, waiting for something to happen. I directed Damian to get the bell from the duffle bag. Still waving the smoking sage, I looked up at the reddening sky. The sun had started to rise.

"Hey, wasn't there an old wives tale that said that red skies rise after an untimely death? I wonder if that's true or has some truth to it," I mused aloud.

"Liam, I love you, but I don't think one death changes the atmosphere or whatever," Damian said, rummaging around until he withdrew the bell.

29

"OK, on my signal, ring the bell," I instructed Damian.

He nodded and looked apprehensive.

"Johanna!" I called out, "Your ghost is no longer welcome here. You need to leave now."

I looked pointedly at Damian, who rang the bell once. Instantly, a whirl of black immerged from the grave, the air turning icy cold. I could no longer see Damian in the sudden haze.

"Hey, Damian, what's happening? Do you need help?" I called out but heard no response. I moved in his direction and saw him on the ground, a dark figure sitting on his stomach, holding him down, choking him.

I acted fast, reached for one of the salt containers, and opened the spout. "Hey, you ugly bitch!" I shouted, making the spectral figure look up, its face hideous and contorted. I flung the container forward, sea salt crystals flying at the ghost, making it bellow and dissipate, freeing my brother.

Damian gasped for air, and I ran to his side, helping him up.

"That witch bitch is angry! We gotta move fast!" I said hurriedly, helping him to his feet and running back to the duffel, but before I could grab the contents, I was strong-armed. I hit the ground hard, coughing as I had been completely winded. I felt pressure upon my chest and then pain, as it felt like five daggers were slowly driving into my skin. The witch's ghost had pinned me to the ground, her nails digging into my abdomen, scratching me, trying to burrow beneath my flesh.

I could hear Damian scream overhead, and I heard the witch say something, and Damian was flung backward. I screamed in agony as she continued to torture me, to drive her grip in deeper.

Her unearthly voice filled the air as the wind swirled all around us. Her eyes glowed with a hellfire red as she drew her horrible face closer to mine. *"You are now MINE,"* she cackled. I could feel my blood begin to trickle down my side, could feel nothing but pain as she kept working her way in. Her free hand then came to my neck, wringing it tightly, closing my windpipe. This was it...this was the end.

And then the wind ceased suddenly, which seemed to catch the witch's ghost off guard as she too seemed surprised. But then the wind was back, strong, strong enough to force her off of my body. I gasped out as I could breathe again, rolling onto my stomach. I saw Damian only a few feet away, and I crawled to him.

When I reached my brother, we shielded our eyes from the winds, looking at where they came from and seeing that they were coming from the lake. Two small figures stood at the water's edge, holding hands, their white eyes glowing in the distance.

"*Mommy…*" they called, flickering, drawing closer.

In a flash, they were there, both of them. Eleanor and Edward, as child ghosts, stood between Damian and me and the witch, and the witch actually looked terrified.

"*You are a very naughty mommy, and naughty mommy's need to be punished.*" The children said in unison.

"*Please, I beg of you…no…*" the witch's ghost pleaded, but her cries fell on deaf ears. The children launched themselves at her, wrapping their arms around her as she screamed. They dragged her down and pulled her towards the lake and under the water, and then all was silent again.

Damian and I were both breathing quickly, looking at each other and then launching ourselves towards the grave. I grabbed the remaining sea salt and doused the grave without any hesitation. I laid the bundle of burning sage on top for good measure, but I could already tell our work was done.

"Is she gone? She won't be coming back?" Damian asked me.

I looked at him and nodded, just as some of the brush on top of the grave caught fire from the burning sage. Large flames sprang up, crackling merrily as they burned, and from the lake, I could have sworn I heard an agonizing scream come from deep below the surface.

30

Tired, we both packed up our things and headed back to the car, silently driving back to the motel to get cleaned up.

After my shower, I stared at my reflection, looking over the marks that had been left behind as gruesome souvenirs. The wounds still stung, but I had made it out alive. I had made it out alive a few times. I had nearly died at least twice in the last twelve hours, and yet...somehow, now I felt better. Now, with the witch taken care of, everything felt settled.

I dressed quickly and came out into our shared room, hearing Damian on the phone with the client who had hired us. I listened as he explained the details of our nightly adventures, with some apparent gaps withheld. He explained that the job was complete and that Camp Hollyfalls was no longer dangerous before hanging up and giving me a significant look.

"So, our first official case is complete, and we have one very satisfied customer," he exclaimed, sitting himself down on his bed with a smile.

"Hey so, who was our client anyway? Didn't you say it was the parents of one of the kids who went missing?" I asked.

"Well yeah, it was, and those parents also happened to be the current owners of Camp Hollyfalls. Funny how that all works out, right?" Damian said with a grin, "and they paid a pretty price to have this all sorted out for them."

I ran a towel through my hair as I, too, sat on my bed, letting out a groan as my weight hit the pillows. "Our first case, closed…it feels good, I guess," I said as I laid back, getting comfortable.

"I am glad to hear you say that because I already have a new client lined up. So, get this, there's this all girl's catholic college that some brutal nun from the 50s supposedly haunts. One of the students wants to pay us to—" Damian suddenly stopped talking, his eyes fixed on the window to our room.

"What? What's the matter?" I asked, going to the window to look. Damian did not speak; he only got to his feet and ran barefoot out the door to our parked car. I was confused but followed him, my bare feet padding against the pavement as I chased my brother over to our car.

"Damian, what's going on?" I asked as I caught up, watching as Damian quickly scanned the area.

"Damian!" I yelled at him again, shocking him out of his state, making him finally look at me.

"Liam, someone was just here! Someone in like, a long coat and sunglasses! They were by the car, they leaned on it—."

"So they were rude? Big deal."

"No, it's not that. It's just that I think they knew who the car belonged to. I think they knew it was ours." Damian said.

My first thought, sadly, was that my brother sounded crazy. "Damian, let's just head back to the room, man. I think you need some sleep and maybe some water," I said, thinking that he was sleep-deprived and probably dehydrated.

"Liam, no—" and then he gasped, heading to the car and lifting one of the windshield wipers, withdrawing a small piece of paper that had been nestled under the blade.

"Where did—" I started, but Damian quickly unfolded the note and began reading aloud.

"Hansel and Gretel,

Good job on the Hollyfalls case. It seems you two have more guile than I thought. If you want to know what really happened to your parents, you need to follow the breadcrumbs. Not everything is as it seems.

41 – 78"

When Damian stopped reading, he looked up at me quizzically.

"Liam…" he said slowly, looking over the note again, before trying to speak. "Liam, do you think…well, what do you think?"

I took the note from his hands to look it over myself. It was cryptic, mysterious, and altogether eerie. Someone knew us, knew our lives, knew about our parents, and knew what we had been up to. Someone was following us, watching us, or maybe even watching us at this very moment.

I nodded my head back towards our room and hurried inside, closing the door swiftly behind Damian when he entered.

"I think someone is watching us, that's for sure," I said, locking the door and fastening the chain and deadbolt. "Someone has been watching us for some time."

"But…the thing about our parents? What do you think that's about? Do you think that maybe, those things never ate them? That maybe there's…there might be a chance that our parents—."

I could hear the hope in Damian's voice, and I wasn't sure if we should entertain it or not. What if the note was true? What if our parents had not been eaten by those ghosts or ghouls or whatever macabre thing we had encountered? What if they were actually…

"What? Do you think that they could still be alive?" I asked, my voice wavering slightly. Damian looked at me with the same expression that I was sure I wore upon my own face. There was confusion and pain, but also that sort of glint that maybe, just maybe, our family could still be put back together.

"OK, let's not get our hopes up or anything. What about this number at the end? 41 – 78. What do you think that means?" I asked, pulling out the note and looking at it again.

"Years? Or page numbers? I don't know. It's pretty vague." Damian said as he looked it over. "Maybe our dear friend Google has something to say about this," Damian said as he turned to his laptop again, typing in the numbers and sifting through the results. All sorts of things came up – math problems, bible verses, nothing helpful.

"Hey, what are these little smudges next to the numbers on the paper?" I asked, pointing at them. They looked initially like just random dots of ink, but I wondered if they were there on purpose.

"Do you think it could be forty-one degrees by seventy-eight degrees?" Damian asked curiously.

"Like weather?" I asked, though immediately feeling stupid.

"No, like coordinates. Forty-one degrees by seventy-eight degrees would be the coordinates of a place, and—" he typed the coordinates in and immediately got a hit, "a place called Deliverance, Pennsylvania. I mean, I'm not really a betting man, Liam, but I'd bet all the money in the world that this is what the note meant. I think we need to set sail for this place, Deliverance."

I sat back on my bed, running a hand over the spot where the ghost had scratched me, had buried her claws into me, and had left me injured. It had been horrible and terrifying, but I had survived. Was it possible that our parents had been able to do the same thing? Could they have?

"So, what do you reckon?" Damian asked me, his face expectant as he looked up from his computer screen. He had a look on his face that simply read, 'we're doing this, and I don't care what you think,' but I wanted him to say it aloud.

"What do I reckon about what?" I asked.

Damian nodded at the computer and then looked back at me, "Do you think we should go take a look? See what's the buzz on Deliverance?"

I bit my lip as I mulled it over, thinking of what had happened and what could happen, and slowly I nodded my head.

"I think that Deliverance might have answers, and that's worth the drive alone."

"You hear that?" Damian shouted, loud enough for someone to hear from outside the room, "The Sullivans are headed for Deliverance!"

III

31

When I came to, the first sensation that hit me was the feeling of cold dirt pouring into the shallow grave. After that, an avalanche of pain.

Every part of me ached. My brain sent a signal down to my limbs as if to confirm that they still worked, but I could not will them into action.

In some ways, the pain greeted me like an old friend. Not the physical pain, but the emotional kind that exploded tenfold in the past twenty-four hours, turning my entire world into hell on Earth.

I opened my eyes and saw the glistening full moon partially visible behind the mass of trees. I wondered if werewolves were roaming about the forest. An absurd thought, but after everything I had uncovered, I wouldn't be surprised.

There was a strange, haunting beauty to the world around me. It was as though now that there was nothing left to torment me, I could finally appreciate the world in what little time I had left.

I tried to speak, to plead for help, but what passed through my lips was a series of rough, scratchy noises, as though my throat had been scraped raw.

Another layer of dirt fell on top of me. Some of it landed in my mouth.

I made the decision not to die here and now. I pulled myself up, the dirt falling away as I rose, looking my would-be killer in the face...only to see my brother Damian staring back at me.

32

THREE DAYS EARLIER...

Neither of us had spoken for the entirety of the car ride. We were still going over the events of how our last case had ended in our heads, the sheer unbelievability of everything that had transpired.

When we saw the road sign that said DELIVERANCE – 10 MILES, we knew we couldn't put it off any longer.

"You know, we could always phone in for assistance?" suggested Damian, even though it wasn't so much a suggestion as it was a cry for help.

I chuckled, trying to insert some humor into the otherwise grim atmosphere. "Sadly, I never got around to checking out the Directory for Supernatural Shit. We try talking about this to anybody, and they will assume that we're either insane, high...or insanely high."

"I know," said Damian. "That's why I've been thinking we need someone who has already been through the wringer. I thought that maybe we could get in touch with Meredith?"

"No. Absolutely not," I said, shutting down the idea then and there.

"She understands better than anyone what we're going through," protested Damian. "She's the only person I can talk to who can help me make sense of all this stuff."

"Listen to me, Damian," I said, adopting an authoritative tone, the age gap between us forgotten. "We're heading into uncharted territory. We have no idea what will await us when we get there. For all we know, this could be a suicide mission. I hope it isn't because I, for one, have no intention of dying in Deliverance." I glanced out the window at the grim landscape surrounding us. "If we're gonna die, I would prefer that we die somewhere more scenic."

"I think we're a little too young to be thinking of that," said Damian shakily.

"Mom and Dad weren't exactly in the autumn of their lives, and they certainly didn't," I said, instantly regretting my sudden harshness.

Damian sighed, not appreciating that I wouldn't take the hint. "I know that I've been instrumental in setting us down this path, but I'm having second thoughts. Maybe we shouldn't be doing this, Liam."

"Why not?"

"Why do you think? Same reasons we don't want Meredith to get involved."

My thoughts drifted to the mysterious note that had spurred this spontaneous journey:

"If you want to know what really happened to your parents, you need to follow the breadcrumbs. Not everything is as it seems. 41 − 78."

"Damian. This is the only way we're going to get to the truth of what happened to our parents. We figured out that the 41 – 78 clue means Deliverance. We're on the right path; I can feel it. We could finally get the answers we've both been waiting for." I implored, puzzling at his change of heart and needing him to want it as much as I did.

Damian kept his eyes on the road, even though he looked as though he wanted to take his hands off the wheel and shake some sense into me. "Liam, I say this with a great deal of respect and love," he said evenly. "But have you ever considered the remote possibility that it might be better if we *don't* find out?"

I blinked, disbelieving I was hearing these words from my brother of all people. "Have you had some kind of brain transplant or something? We both need answers, Damian. We can't go through life not knowing. We've tried that approach for the last few decades and look how well that worked out. I'm an obsessive-compulsive mess, and you struggle to hold down a job. We have both been scarred by losing mom and dad. Do you ever wonder what life could have been like had they actually lived? If they had shown us how to grow up? Gone through all the rites of passage a parent should do rather than leave us hurtling from one disaster to the next? Maybe we'd have turned out more well-adjusted. Maybe even have kids of our own. And, most importantly, we'd be able to go through life without having to see a single ghost!"

"You know, I thought that, too," said Damian, his voice shaky. "I thought that getting all the answers would change everything, would give me and you proper closure. But when I look back on all those years we missed them, all those years not knowing what happened to them...I still had room in my heart for hope. But if we do this, we won't be able to hope anymore. We will have to live with the truth of it. And I don't know if we'll be able to."

"You really think the truth is going to be that bad?"

"Liam. Our last two cases involved mass cannibalism and a horde of missing children at a demented camp. You think that just because those families had closure, the nightmare was over for them? If anything, they now have to live with the knowledge that their loved ones died under horrific circumstances."

I couldn't understand where this burst of pessimism was coming from. "OK," I said, trying to play along. "So, what exactly do you think is going to happen when we get there?"

"Two possible things," announced Damian. "One: we won't find anything connected to mom and dad. That the cryptic note someone left us was little more than an elaborate hoax set up by some jerk with far too much time on their hands. Two: we will find out the truth, and it will provide the fuel for another decade's worth of nightmares."

"Well, thank God you're here to keep things optimistic," I said sardonically. "You forget, Damian, that we've stared death in the face, not once, but twice. And unless this is hell, which looking around here wouldn't really surprise me, we are still very much alive. So, we must have been doing something right. Just think, after we solve this case, we don't ever have to go near another ghost, ghoul, or lunatic ever again. We can live normal lives. I've seen how close you and Meredith were getting," I added teasingly. "Maybe there could even be the sound of wedding bells in the future."

"Last time I checked, you weren't a clairvoyant," said Damian. "Meredith and I like each other, but I don't think we're anywhere near that stage yet."

"Doesn't mean you won't be," I said. "Just try to picture the idea of you two living a normal life, having all the things that people are supposed to have."

"But Liam..." questioned Damian. "What if we're too screwed up to enjoy those things?"

That question stopped me in my tracks. I had been asking myself that same question over and over, and I still didn't have a convincing answer.

We continued the drive in silence, trying to push any thoughts of the future out of our heads and focus on the task at hand.

As the town ahead began to take form, I couldn't help but wonder if we had actually died on one of our previous endeavors and were now entering hell.

33

The entire town reminded me of my dad's old pocket watch.

He said it had belonged to my grandad, and always used to carry it with him. Then, one day, it stopped, the hands permanently fixed at seven minutes past five. I had asked my dad why he had never bothered to get it fixed, why he seemed content to keep it as it was, permanently frozen in time.

My dad had replied, "Because there's a certain beauty in things that never change."

At the time, I was too young to appreciate what he meant by those words. Only when I looked back on them as a young man did I start to appreciate the sentiment.

Deliverance had that look and feel of a town that had, like the watch, frozen in time. But there was nothing beautiful to be found here.

As we drove into town, we saw crackling neon signs that wouldn't have looked out of place in the 1980s, but today, seemed like relics.

The few people we glimpsed walking down the street were dressed in an array of fashions, as though they hadn't decided from which generation they had heralded.

The sun had long since settled over the town, giving the buildings the look of a sea of grey stretching out down the road.

"Any idea what we're walking into?" asked Damian.

"Not particularly," I said, taking in the clashing aesthetics.

"Well, I'm certainly not doing any detective work on an empty stomach," announced Damian. "I could murder a burger right now."

I looked at Damian, feeling relieved. "That's the most sensible thing you've said all day."

It had been my mom that had started the burger routine.

When I had first been diagnosed with obsessive-compulsive disorder, I was too caught up in my own little world to care what other people thought of me, which made me an easy target for kids at school.

I remember having a set of pencils lined up in a specific sequence, moving through the colors of the rainbow, or organized from smallest to largest. I found pride in those patterns.

But the other kids caught on. First, it had started with them rearranging my pencils before snapping them in front of me, labeling me a freak.

I remember having a massive tantrum in the middle of the classroom, which, while not unheard of for a six-year-old, was still quite extreme. Extreme enough for my mom to come to the school to talk to the teachers.

After the incident, I had thought that she was going to scream her head off at me or tell me how disappointed she was.

Instead, she had driven to pick Damian up from football practice and taken us to a local burger joint, buying each of us a double bacon cheeseburger. She then sat us down to talk about how things had been going for me at school and how we needed to get help for my diagnosis. Damian, ever my protector even then, needed no convincing whatsoever.

And then Mom had said, "Throughout life, when you feel like life is getting on top of you, or there are things that you want to let out without screaming at the rest of the world, go and grab a burger. It'll be a good bonding session for you both."

And that was a tradition that Damian and I maintained long into adulthood. Whenever we made a plan of attack for anything difficult, it always started with burgers and fries.

We sat down at a local bar which was unlike anything we had ever seen. The entire bar was adorned with crosses and beads, containing what looked like trinkets from every single religion known to man.

"Don't think I've ever been in a religious bar before," said Damian as the waitress delivered our food.

"Deliverance is a very spiritual place," said the waitress, slightly perturbed as though insulted by Damian's statement. "The local church has been good to us, keeping us clothed and fed, ensuring that we are always wealthy. Our faith in their work isn't much to ask for in return."

At that point, I noticed everyone in the bar was sneaking looks at us, the clear outsiders in this hive mind of believers.

Trying to ease some of the tension, I asked, "We're hoping to find a place to stay for the night. Do you think you can direct us to a decent motel?"

The waitress looked at me quizzingly, as though I had just grown a third eye. "Oh, we don't have motels in Deliverance."

"So, there's nowhere we can stay?" asked Damian, now eager to tuck into his burger.

"Oh, I didn't say that," said the waitress. "All visitors can find accommodation at the Sainthood Church."

"The Sainthood Church?" I repeated, unable to contain my bafflement.

"Yes. Minister Deacon believes that all who come through Deliverance are lost souls looking to accept God into their lives and need spiritual guidance. There is no fee for a night's stay, for you cannot put a price on spirituality."

"That'd make a good slogan," said Damian, chuckling.

The waitress smiled, but it didn't quite meet her eyes. "You can head over there when you're finished. But be warned. Minister Deacon will want to check you both to make sure that you two are... worthy."

And she turned on her heels, leaving us both alone in the booth.

"So, what are you thinking?" I asked.

"Avoid eye contact and quote the Bible if confronted," replied Damian, and I couldn't tell if he was being serious or not.

"No, I mean about accommodation. I don't like the idea of not having personal space."

Damian shrugged. "Well, there is the car, but if the claustrophobia doesn't keep us awake, my snoring definitely will."

"So..." I said. "Off to Sainthood. It would be interesting to hear what they do with sinners."

34

W e parked the car down the street from the Church and headed towards the entrance, the cold night air biting at us, the idea of a warm bed in the Church becoming increasingly inviting.

When we laid eyes on Sainthood, we weren't quite sure what to expect. Given the somewhat-dilapidated state of the rest of the town, we were anticipating a church crumbling from within, showing its age.

But, if anything, the church appeared to be the most well-maintained building in the entire town. The walls were a fresh cream, the paint glistening as though recently coated, the windows newly installed. For all we knew, the church could have been built just yesterday.

We stepped inside and walked into the sight of a prayer taking place.

But it was unlike any prayer we had ever seen. The practitioners kneeled on a stone floor, chanting in unison. It was difficult to grasp what language they were speaking, but it certainly wasn't anything Damian and I were familiar with.

At the back of the hall stood a woman. She was dressed majestically in purple robes, her auburn hair pulled back in a ponytail, with a face that appeared to be completely stoic, save for the eyes that glistened with manic energy as she took in the sights before her.

Noticing us, she held up a hand, and the prayer immediately ceased. She walked down the center of the hall, her robes trailing behind her, giving the impression that she could have been gliding through the air.

Finally, she came to a halt in front of us.

"Good evening, gentleman," she said warmly, offering a hand. I took it, surprised by the heat generating from her, as though she had been living on a volcano. "My name is Debra Deacon, and I am the First Minister of this church. It is a pleasure to welcome you both to my domain. Are you here looking for spiritual awakening?"

"Actually... we're looking for a place to stay for the night," said Damian, who clearly didn't want to be roped into any prayers.

Deacon's smile remained etched on her face, despite a notable twitch. Damian's words were evidently not the answer she had been hoping for but one she accepted, nonetheless.

"In that case, welcome. I'll show you to your rooms," she said, waving a hand and beckoning for us to follow her.

As we left the main hall, I noticed one of the practitioners, an older man in his seventies, looking at us quizzically, but he had disappeared from view before I could take anything else in.

Deacon directed us up the stairs to a row of beds, a few already occupied by sleeping forms.

"We have two at the end available for the night," she said. "Might I ask your names?"

I was about to reply when Damian said, "Jonas. And this is my best mate, Andrew."

"Might I ask what you both do for a living?" asked Deacon.

"We're traveling salesman," said Damian, and understanding the need to look authentic, I tried not to burst into laughter. "We travel the country convincing people to invest in our top-of-the-line vacuum cleaners. So, you could say we're in the same line of work. We both sway people to our causes somewhat."

"I wouldn't make such a comparison," said Deacon. "What we do is for the good of the soul, to help people move towards the better versions of themselves. Now, there is no fee for your stay, but I must ask you to participate in morning prayers. Think of it as religious therapy."

"We can manage that," I said. "I don't know if Jonas and I are really the spiritual types."

"My dears," said Deacon. "Everyone has the capacity for spiritual awakening. You just need to leave the correct breadcrumbs for them to follow."

It was a good thing she turned away and left us when she did because otherwise, she would have seen the shock and horror on our faces.

Could Deacon have written the note that led us to Deliverance?

35

Sleep felt just out of grasp, and the night was restless. It was as though we had been allocated the kind of beds designed to prevent sleep.

I couldn't stop thinking about the last words Deacon had said to us.

It couldn't be her. It just couldn't be.

But at the same time, I had no reason to think otherwise. I was beginning to think that maybe Damian was right, and coming here was not the most brilliant idea.

But Deacon seemed like an ordinary priest. Perhaps a little overzealous, but there didn't appear to be anything supernatural about her.

As if in response to my thoughts, I heard the creaking of floorboards and the straining of age-old springs as somewhere in the dark, someone shuffled out of bed.

I couldn't see who it was, the dark failing to adjust to my eyes. I looked over at Damian's bed. He was clearly fast asleep, the light snoring giving him away.

Instead, I relied on my ears to paint the picture for me. I could hear footsteps shuffling across the room, unhooking the latch on the doorway and pulling the door open with a prolonged creak, as though the unseen insomniac was trying to wake the dead.

Assuming the dead hadn't awakened him.

As the door opened, there was a flicker of light, faintly illuminating the previously-black sleeping quarters. I could make out the burly figure of a man, and with it, his face.

His face was what unnerved me most of all. The way he gazed absently into the doorway... I tried to think of a better word than resignation.

He shuffled into the corridor, every step dragging like a man on the way to his execution.

He didn't close the door behind him, leaving it slightly ajar. A part of me wanted to follow him, to place the source of his acceptance, but I had had enough experience of rushing into things without knowing exactly what I was getting into to stay put.

So I stayed in bed and listened, trying to let my imagination paint the scene that may or may not be happening downstairs.

I could hear voices. At least I thought I heard voices. One of the voices was Deacon's, but the other sounds were more like echoes. They could be coming from anywhere... or nowhere, as though they were seeping through the walls of the building.

Now they grew louder, only this time not speaking in English, but in a language I couldn't place, rising in pitch and volume, taking on a guttural sound.

And then there was a scream, exploding throughout the entire building, penetrating the air. It was a cry that carried the power of several decades' worth of pain. I tried to think of every possible reason for the screaming, every vile thing on Earth that could prompt such a response.

And yet I knew my imagination would fall short.

The light was shifting in color, no longer a dim yellow, but a dark blue, almost ethereal, like a gas. There was something quite hypnotizing and beautiful about it. I could gaze into it for hours.

But the spell was quickly broken by the sound of another voice. And this one haunted me like no other voice could.

"Liam..."

It was a voice I knew instantly. A voice that I had heard so many times before that no matter how long it had been since I last heard it, it would always be with me as clear as day.

It was my mother's voice.

"Leave," the whisper pleaded, as though it was straining to speak.

"Mom?" I said into the darkness, as though expecting a back-and-forth conversation.

"Leave NOW!" my mom's voice rang out, taking on a lower pitch, becoming almost demonic in delivery. And suddenly, it felt as though she was right in front of me, her hands gripping my shoulders like she used to do to calm me down from an OCD-induced fit...

...I sat upright in bed, screaming, my body soaked in sweat.

My eyes darted around the room, trying to find the source of anything unnatural, but nobody was there—just a row of beds full of unperturbed sleeping forms.

I looked over at the open door, the only physical evidence of the mysterious goings-on, but the door was firmly shut.

My brain immediately started trying to rationalize what I had just seen.

Maybe it had all been just a dream. After all, if something like that had really happened, surely it would have woken up the entire church. I glanced at Damian, still fast asleep in bed, none the wiser.

Deciding it was preferable to dismiss the entire event as a dream, I settled back to sleep, trying to push the specter of doubt out of my mind.

36

We woke just after 7 am. Living a semi-nomadic lifestyle had screwed up our sleeping patterns, but at least we still possessed the discipline to rise early.

Damian sat up in bed, yawning. "Sleep well?" he asked, utterly oblivious to my night-time experience.

Part of me wondered whether I should tell him about what I had seen that night. Tell him about the man who left the room, the man whom, by my guessing, wasn't present among the risers this morning. Tell him about the blue light and the screams. If we were going to make it through this alive, I felt I needed to make him aware of the danger we were facing.

But that would also mean telling him about mom. It would mean telling him about hearing her voice. And despite his dismissive attitude on the journey down here, I could tell Damian yearned for answers just as much as I did.

But that longing could make him reckless, more inclined to take significant risks. And there was always the possibility of word getting back to Deacon. Whatever her involvement in this event, I felt that the less she knew, the better.

"I've had better nights," I admitted.

We got out of bed and hit the showers. I let the lukewarm water run over me as though it would cleanse me of all I had seen the night before.

We went downstairs into the main hall where Deacon was already setting up the church. She looked as fresh-faced as ever, not a hair out of place, as though this put-together appearance was in a permanent state of preservation.

"Good morning, gentlemen," she offered courteously. "I trust you had a pleasant night's sleep?"

"Very good, thank you," said Damian. His stomach made a loud grumble, prompting his next question. "I hope I'm not being cheeky, but you wouldn't happen to have any breakfast around here, would you?"

Deacon raised an eyebrow. "Oh, we don't start the day with breakfast," she said matter-of-factly. "Here at Sainthood, we believe that a meal has to be earned before it can be enjoyed."

"And how might we earn it?" I asked.

"By joining us in the morning prayer," replied Deacon. "We commence in ten minutes." She took a few steps, attending to the altar, when she turned back and said, "Oh, by the way, gentlemen, I might be able to bring some business your way."

"Oh?" I asked, caught off-guard.

"Yes, we could do with a new vacuum cleaner for the church," said Deacon. "I'm sure you understand; cleanliness is next to godliness. So, perhaps you could show me a sample of your product. I assure you I will make it worth your while."

Damian and I exchanged nervous glances. It was supposed to be a harmless untruth. Neither of us could have predicted she would pull the thread.

Thankfully, Damian stepped in. "We don't have our stock on us at the moment," he said. "We have a supplier who ships them out to us when we're looking at making a profit."

Deacon nodded slowly. "Fair enough," she said to our surprise. "Assuming you'll be with us for the next few days, I'm sure we can work something out."

And she turned away, continuing to prepare the church for the morning services. I wanted to pat Damian on the shoulder and say, "Well done" for thinking of something on the spot, but I didn't want to risk saying or doing anything that could get back to Deacon's scrutinizing eyes and ears.

Sure enough, within ten minutes, the entire church was gathered in the main hall, with Deacon standing at the altar. Damian and I took seats at the back of the room partly to put some distance between Deacon and us and partly to give us a quick exit if we needed to head for the door.

It wasn't until everybody was seated that we noticed the abnormality of the set-up.

The entire church was seated on the right side of the hall, leaving the left completely absent. We both wanted to ask about this peculiar setup, but the service had already begun, and we didn't want to risk disrupting.

"My people," said Deacon, speaking with the confidence of a woman who had shepherded thousands of souls over the years. "We are gathered here this morning to bask in the spiritual rewards bestowed upon us by the divine. They may work in mysterious ways, perhaps in ways that seem to harm us. But we must never lose sight of the functions of Sainthood. Wealth, Divineness and Prosperity."

At this point, everyone in the church repeated the last three words en masse as though hypnotized. Damian and I exchanged looks. Neither of us was particularly religious, but we were expecting something along the lines of Christianity. Certainly nothing like this gathering.

"But Divineness is a two-way road, and our riches would not be made possible without those who have crossed over to the other side."

She gestured to the left side of the hall, rife with empty seats. And then she began speaking to them with complete conviction, as though there was an entire audience of people sitting there hanging on her every word. "We thank you, oh bountiful ones, for showing us light in the dark, for offering us solace from the solitude we must endure on this Earth. We thank you for demonstrating the Divine Power to us so that one day, we may know such power ourselves. And in turn, we offer you our souls, oh bountiful ones, a bond between the two worlds that we intend to strengthen with each passing day."

Every participant in the hall was looking at the empty chairs. I couldn't help but wonder if there was some magic trick occuring that I wasn't clued into, a spectator being fooled. But Damian and I followed suit, knowing that the more effort we made to blend in, the less likely Deacon would suspect us.

Except Deacon may not have been our only problem.

Sitting about four rows in front of us, stealing a glance at us from time to time, was a man. And not just any man.

It was the man who had exited the dormitory last night. Seeing him in the light for the first time was odd, but I would know that defeatist expression anywhere.

But now, he was looking at Damian and me with a new look, one that sent chills running through my bones.

Recognition.

37

We left the church later that morning, assuring Deacon that we would return later in the day. "I hope you found our service a spiritual one," she inquired. "One that left you willing to accept God into your heart."

"Yeah, about that," said Damian. "What kind of God was that meant to be? My religious education is a little rusty, but I don't think I've ever come across a sermon like that."

"My dear fellow," responded Deacon. "God is a large, unwieldy, and encompassing subject. God provides his teachings through Christianity, Buddhism, Hinduism, and many more avenues. As a young girl, I believed that there was a specific God and only one way to worship him. But I have discovered over the years that God is ultimately interpretation."

She looked at us speculatively, and then continued. "You look at many other establishments around the world and see that God has a very loose grip on these organizations. This occurs because people have deluded themselves into thinking they don't need God in their lives because God has been watered down by the varying faiths. My church combines them all. No one is exempt from Divineness. We won't turn away people based on background as we believe we are all truly God's Children. I didn't have much in the way of faith, until I was introduced to a Divine power with proof that God is working among us, sending his Sentries to do his bidding."

"Sentries?" repeated Damian.

"Those who have yet to pass on. Those who are still among us today. The spirits who were in attendance with us today."

I tried to control my facial expressions. "So, the spirits were seated on the left side of the church?" I asked, saying it out loud, hoping it would make sense in my head. But it only served to confuse me further.

"Precisely," said Deacon. "Souls that have yet to pass by into the next world and have unfinished business to attend to. Many of today's service attendees all know at least one person who is not yet at peace. It is our job to help those souls find peace. I'm sure you both know somebody who was taken before their time and felt the flicker of recognition as they refused to move on, in part because they knew they still had to do right by you."

I audibly gulped, wondering how much truth there was in Deacon's words.

Sensing my discomfort, Damian took me by the arm and said, "Well, First Minister, you've certainly given us plenty of food for thought. And we'll be sure to learn more from you upon our return. But for now, we need to go and check-in regarding our stock supplies."

And with that, he led me out of the church. We could both feel Deacon's eyes burning into us as she watched us depart.

We didn't know where else to go. It was clear enough that Deacon's influence ran deep throughout the town. There didn't appear to be anywhere we could go without the possibility of one of her followers getting back to her with word of our true intentions.

"So, what are your thoughts?" I asked.

"Either that woman knows how to spin a good yarn," said Damian. "Or she genuinely buys into this spiritual crap."

"It's not possible," I said, feeling as though I was clinging to reason by my fingernails.

"Liam, I think the concept of what is possible and what isn't is in flux with us both," said Damian.

Knowing the immense risk I was taking, I took a deep breath and said, "Damian, last night... I think I heard mom."

Damian skidded to a halt on the pavement. "What?"

"I heard her voice last night, along with a strange blue light," I continued. We stood on the sidewalk as I filled him in on everything that had taken place the night before.

"And you're only telling me this now?" asked Damian, sounding affronted.

"I didn't know what we were dealing with!" I said. "For all I knew, it might have been a dream or something. It wasn't until I saw the same guy in service this morning that I figured it had to be real. But I couldn't say anything with Deacon hanging over us like an overgrown bat! I'm not even sure what I'm supposed to have seen!"

"How do I know you're not just saying this just to get me to stay?" asked Damian, his tone accusatory.

"What do you mean?"

"We both know that this whole adventure is for your benefit rather than mine. I told you it would be better just to walk away, forget the whole thing. But you seemed determined to stick it out, didn't you? So how do I know you won't say anything just to keep me on the case?"

"That's bullshit!" I protested. "And if you get your head out of your ass, you'll work that out! I have never lied to you, Damian. And I never will. I want to find out what happened to Mom and Dad, but I wouldn't sacrifice you to get there!"

Damian's silence hurt more than anything he might have said in response.

"My God," I said. "You actually think that, don't you? You really think I am so busy chasing after the family I lost that I'd gladly throw away the family I have left?"

"Frankly, I don't know what you think anymore," said Damian and picked up the pace, leaving me standing on the street corner.

"Where are you going?" I called after him.

"For a walk to clear my head," said Damian. "I'll see you back at the church later."

And then he disappeared around a street corner and out of sight. I wanted to chase after him and tell him that there was no truth to his words, but I held myself back.

Another part of me wanted to stick this out, whatever it took. We were so close to finding out the truth. We might never get another shot at this.

But before I could muse on these thoughts any further, someone approached me from across the street. It was the man who had been eyeballing us in the church.

Seeing him standing before me, up close, he looked as though he had aged a decade in a matter of days, heavy bags under his eyes, his face gaunt, his hair an unkempt mess.

"You're Liam, aren't you?" he asked in a shaky voice.

Thinking it safer to play the fool, I responded with, "I have no idea what you're talking about."

"You don't fool me," said the man. "You look so much like Derrick."

"Derrick," I repeated, no longer caring about any pretense, just feeling a deep hunger for the truth. "You knew my father?"

"Years ago," said the man. "My name is Arnold. We were friends... more or less. At least as close to friends as Minister Deacon would allow it."

"Deacon? Does she know anything about my dad?"

But Arnold shook his head. "You really have no idea what's going on, do you? You should not have come back here."

"What do you mean 'back here?' This is our first visit to Deliverance."

"Listen," said Arnold, his voice a low whisper, as though conscious of unseen spies in the street. "I can't do anything to help the pair of you. But I'm begging you now. Find your brother and go home. Forget all about this place."

"I've spent years looking for the truth," I replied. "And you're asking me just to walk away from the whole thing?"

"It's what your parents would have wanted. You do it for them if you can't do it for yourselves. You were lucky the first time. You might not be this time." And then he turned on his heel and took off down the street.

"Wait!" I called after him. "How do you know my parents?"

"Know them?" Arnold repeated without turning back. "Your parents and I were part of the same flock. We were members of the Sainthood Church."

He was out of sight before he could answer the bombardment of questions that came rushing to the surface.

38

I couldn't believe it.

Dad, a member of the Sainthood Church?

Dad had always hated religion when we were kids. He once said that "God was for the people who lack the initiative to do anything themselves, kiddo."

Could Deacon have known our parents? It was not possible. By my guesswork, Deacon was around forty years old, so either someone was leading the church before her, or she had managed to age with unnatural grace.

I needed to find Damian and get his opinion on the matter.

I didn't have to search long before I found him sitting on a park bench. I waited for him to shoo me away or tell me to piss off, but he remained silent. So instead, I tentatively took a seat next to him.

For a while, neither of us spoke, clearly not over the hurt. Then, finally, Damian said, "For what it's worth, I don't think you would sell me out. That was just... me being a bit of an ass."

"I know," I said.

"You are the only thing I have left in my life," said Damian. "I know my life hasn't turned out the way I had hoped, but all the hardships I went through were made all the better by having you there with me. I probably wouldn't have made it this far without you."

"Same here, bro," I responded. "I can't think of many people who would tolerate my OCD-crap."

"We've made it this far by looking out for each other," said Damian. "The only way that will still happen is if we continue to do so. We need to trust each other. And you're right. If I upped and walked away from the whole thing, I'd probably spend the rest of my life wondering what might have happened. And it would eat away at me."

"Well, if you're going to take that risk," I said. "It would probably help to know what we're going to be up against."

And then I told him about Arnold, about the warning he had given me, about our parents possible connection to Sainthood Church.

Damian's mouth was hanging open by the time I was finished speaking. Clearly, he was having just as much trouble seeing Dad as a religious fanatic. "I don't want to believe it," he said.

"Neither do I," I said. "But can you think of any other explanation?"

"Trust me, I'm thinking of anything else. How much do we actually know about Sainthood Church?"

"Not much, but they seem to have a wide reach. Unfortunately, everyone in this town seems to have been brainwashed. I don't think we can ask too many questions without this getting back to Deacon."

"Who is this woman, anyway?" asked Damian. "What part does she play in all of this? She can't have anything to do with mom or dad. She's far too young for that. I think we need to speak to this Arnold guy, find out what he knows."

"I thought the same thing," I said. "But he's already taken a big risk talking to me. And I'm guessing Deacon would be more than a little pissed off if she found out. And this time around, I'd rather not leave a trail of corpses in our wake."

"So, we're going straight back into the lion's den?" asked Damian matter-of-factly.

"Pretty much."

"All right," said Damian. "But I want you to promise me one thing; when this is all over, regardless of how it ends, assuming we make it through the whole thing in one piece, we put all of this to rest. Ghosts, demons, whatever you want to call them. I want to go back to the days where the biggest stress was paying my cable bill."

"Deal," I said.

We headed back to the church, trying to steer clear of the other parishioners. Deacon was looking at us with hungry eyes, which settled on us as soon as we entered the room and only averted her gaze after we had left.

We had so many questions swimming around in our heads but no way to get the answers. Arnold was nowhere to be seen for the rest of the day, and both Damian and I wondered what might have happened to him. Perhaps he had decided to take the next bus out of town to escape Deacon's wrath.

Or maybe she had cottoned on to his good Samaritan deed.

We had several more sessions practiced alongside the so-called spirits. But Deacon's words had caused a stir in me. If there were indeed spirits sharing the room space with us, could our parents be among them, watching us from across the room?

We went to bed later that evening, though neither of us could sleep, not when we were sitting on so much knowledge.

Finally, just as it felt like sleep was in reach, a clammy hand gripped my shoulder. I was fully awake as I looked into the panic-stricken face of Arnold.

"I told you you should have left here," he said, wheezing as though his breathing was becoming more hindered with each word he spoke. "Now she'll take you to–"

But before he could say anything else, he doubled over, choking. I had no idea what I was supposed to do.

Suddenly, he stood up straight, as if to attention, and started walking out of the room.

I heard another voice, and it took a few seconds to realize it was coming from Arnold's mouth.

But it wasn't Arnold's voice.

And as I looked closely, I could see some blue mist faintly emitting from around Arnold's head.

As he walked out of the room, stiffly as though he were walking on stilts, I turned over to Damian and shook him awake. "Damian, wake up!"

Damian rolled over on the bed. "If you want to complain about my snoring–"

"Arnold was here. There's something wrong with him. We have to follow him!"

We threw on our clothes, carrying our shoes to offset the creaking of the floorboards.

We followed Arnold down the corridor, making sure to keep some distance between him and us. We realized that we were likely heading into the basement.

As we entered, I had expected the area to be rife with cobwebs, untouched by life. But there was no sense of abandonment in the basement, no dripping from leaky pipes or piles of dust. If anything, it had the feeling of being frequently tended to.

And we were about to see why.

We saw candlelight in the distance, and the outline of several cloaked figures and banners hung back from around the entrance.

Arnold walked into the center of the room, where the lights brightened, revealing a group of people standing in the space around an oak table. All were cloaked.

At the center of the table, with her hood drawn over her head, was Deacon.

"I trust you are finding this body meets your expectations?" asked Deacon.

"Perhaps he is a bit long in the tooth," said Arnold in an un-Arnold voice, a dialect that felt more refined as though it belonged to a different time. "But I'm content with a placeholder for now, as I'm sure you will provide me with a more valuable host in due time."

"That we shall," said Deacon, gesturing to the table. "As I'm sure you will hold up your end of the agreement."

"Worry not. We will happily take a few more years off your clock."

"If you would like to take your place, we can commence with the ceremony."

Arnold did as instructed and lay down on the table while Damian and I watched, fascinated and trying to make sense of the whole situation while contemplating our next move.

"My people," said Deacon, sounding less regal and more demonic. "Our brother has forsaken his soul in place of our historical friend, commencing the Harmonious Ritual of Transferrence. Our brother, who has been with us for decades, will now be forsaken for a greater cause."

She removed something from her robes, and as it glistened, we could see it was a ceremonial dagger.

Before Damian or I had time to react, she raised the dagger upward, with just enough time for Arnold's face of awe and wonder to give way to shock and horror... before she plunged it into his chest.

Arnold screamed as blue mist emitted from the fresh wound, filling the entire room, passing through all its inhabitants.

And then it was gone, just as quickly as it had come.

Arnold sat up on the table, admiring his hands as though he had never used them before. Then, he gestured for Deacon to come forward with a click of his fingers, which she did promptly.

Arnold placed his hands on her shoulders, and we could see blue mist flowing from his body into hers.

Deacon stumbled back, breathing heavily. Her hands went for her face, a quick feel telling her all she needed to know. Then, regaining her bearings, she bowed to Arnold. "Thank you, o bountiful one."

"We will, of course, need fresh hosts soon. I trust you will be able to provide some."

"Oh, worry not," said Deacon. "In fact, I have two fresh specimens that I believe will be to your liking, depending on which ones are ready to re-walk the mortal plane."

Before I had time to register what she had just said, I felt a burly hand on my shoulder. I turned, half expecting it to be Damian, but to my horror, it was a sizeable robed figure, a giant of a man. He didn't say anything, but we knew to make a move would be the end of us.

We had been discovered.

39

I struggled against the ropes now binding my hands as we were escorted deeper into the basement. Once fully inside, we could see that it looked like less of a basement and more like a regal chamber, richly decorated with glistening drapes and golden scriptures. Deacon remained seated, surrounded by hooded acolytes.

We both looked around, searching for any possible means of escape. "I wouldn't bother," said Deacon quickly, as though reading our minds. "The only way out of this room is the way you came in."

"You know, I'm surprised," she continued, tutting as we were thrown before her. "As the sons of Nancy and Derrick Sullivan, I'm genuinely surprised by your lack of tact. Your parents were far more elusive. More so than what I gave them credit for."

"You knew our parents?" I asked. Even when I was facing death, the desire for knowledge overwhelmed any other thoughts of self-preservation.

"Indeed," said Deacon through gritted teeth. "You know, I've known many souls in my 116 years on this planet, but I don't think I've ever met anyone who has had so much to give yet delivered so little."

"116?" Damian repeated. "Are you mad?"

"No, my dear boy," said Deacon. "I am eternal. I have lived through two World Wars, seen the world brought to heel so many times."

"How on earth is that possible?" I asked. "You certainly don't look it, you look–"

And then I got a good look at her face. Whatever Arnold had done to her, the 'years off the clock' expression was not hyperbole. She did indeed look as though she had de-aged by five years. "What did Arnold do to you?"

"You still think that that was Arnold?" asked Deacon, almost incredulous. "Arnold is already dead, which is a shame because he had been one of our most loyal followers for years. But, when he started spreading gossip to you two, I knew that Arnold needed to go. That isn't to say I still couldn't find a use for his body afterward."

"So who is in Arnold right now?" asked Damian, playing along, partly for answers and partly to stall time until we could get an opening to escape.

At this point, Arnold stepped forward. "My name is Stanley Yates," he said. "I was born in Oklahoma, 1933 and died in New York, 1976."

"That's not possible!" I exclaimed.

"Liam," said Deacon coaxingly, like a disappointed teacher speaking to an unruly pupil. "There is no point in trying to lie to me. You have had contact with the supernatural. I can tell, I can see it in your aura."

"Our what?" we both asked in unison, feeling as though she was speaking a different language.

"I have the unique ability to see a person's aura when I meet them. The strength of a person's aura is dependent on their contact with the supernatural. For the most part, people don't have particularly strong auras. You might see a faint blue if someone has had a one-off occurrence with a departed family member. The more experience one has with the supernatural, the brighter the aura, and the stronger the energy. And I must say, the second you two walked into my church, you were so bright, you could have lit up a city block. I didn't want to believe it at first. I had given up all hope of ever coming across you again. Because I had only seen that kind of aura once before, around your parents."

"Why would our parents have anything to do with a psycho like you?" asked Damian, at which point, one of the hooded acolytes slapped Damian hard across the face.

"You two genuinely don't have any idea about your heritage, do you?" asked Deacon. "Your parents came to this church years ago. I can't remember specifically, it may have been late 70s, early 80s. When you've lived for as long as I have, time tends to bleed together."

"Anyway," she continued, "I came to this town as a simple priest looking to promote the word of God. I was a naïve child back then, full of deluded ideals of right and wrong, perfectly content to live in my elemental world."

"But that's when I had my first contact with the Restless; spirits who refused to move on. I believe the first one I ever came across was a child murderer executed by lethal injection. And he was not alone. There was a legion of spirits who felt that their time on this planet was unfinished, that they could still do so much to and for the world."

"They needed spiritual guidance. The Restless required someone to find useless bodies for them, people who wouldn't be missed, the homeless, immigrants. Of course, as time went on, it was no longer enough just to have a new lease on life. We needed to capture people of influence, people with money and power. So, we targeted the elite of the world, the people who had decided to forgo God in favor of living in their corporate heaven."

"Which is how you have managed to finance this den," observed Damian.

"Deliverance was the place where I had my true awakening. I have a kinship with this town."

"So, what do you get out of this?" I asked. "What's to stop one of these bastards from taking over you?"

Deacon held up her hand, revealing a ring set with a large emerald gem. "The Ring of the Anointed," explained Deacon. "I discovered it among several other trinkets. As long as I have this, I am exempt from their takeover. And besides, I am the one who finds fresh bodies for them to inhabit. They need me."

"This is all a very educational experience," said Damian dryly. "But you still haven't told us; where do our parents fit into this holy hell?"

"Your parents were part of the church," said Deacon. "They supported me in my mission. They were both young and needed guidance, looking to me, yearning to be a part of something greater than themselves." She leaned in close, saying the words that would wound more than any blow. "We were like family."

"You're lying!" I shouted, fighting against the acolyte's seemingly iron grip. "Our parents would never have had anything to do with someone like you!"

"Oh, but they did. For many years, in fact. Until they slinked off in the middle of the night, like rats in the dark. But I wasn't about to let such a slight go unpunished. I tracked them down."

"And you killed them?" I asked. It slipped out, a question I had been waiting my whole life to ask. I felt terrified now that it was finally going to be answered.

"They were traitors to Sainthood. I couldn't let such a slight go unpunished. I didn't bother with you boys because I figured your parents would have tried to brainwash you into believing their chosen reality."

"But news travels fast and wide, and I heard about your latest adventures. And that was when I realized that you had inherited your parents' knack for catching onto the supernatural. The energy you two would have emitted, the lifeforce I would have been granted if I had given you up as hosts."

"So, it was you who wrote the note?" asked Damian.

"I did. I knew you would not pass up the opportunity to uncover what happened to your parents, and you wouldn't even care that you could be walking into a trap. So, here we are."

I felt a numbness wash over me. I finally had all the answers I could have wanted, but I found myself wishing I could erase it all from my memory.

"Now, we can decide which souls will take on your bodies. It's a shame your parents aren't here. I would have loved to have the whole set."

"I wouldn't bet on that," said one of the acolytes holding Damian. To our – and Deacon's surprise – the acolyte released Damian, pulling the ropes around his hands loose as he did so, and began attacking the other hooded figures. He turned to Damian and yelled, "Run, kiddo! Run for your lives!"

At the sound of the word 'kiddo', I was suddenly ten years old again. "Dad?" I breathed.

"We don't have much time!" said another acolyte, wrestling with the group while Deacon took a step back, determined to keep herself away from the conflict.

Not needing to be told twice, Damian untied my hands, and then we sprinted for the exit, up the stairs, back into the main hall and bolted for the front door.

Once outside, we darted around, frantic that someone was going to apprehend us. Anyone could be an enemy waiting to pounce.

So Damian and I continued to run. Finally, after so many years spent chasing the truth, now we were running away from it. The irony was clearly not lost on Damian either. "I bet you're thrilled we came here now!" he exclaimed between breaths.

We darted into the woods on the edge of town, the only place where we could possibly lose our pursuers. I lost track of how long we had been running. It could have been for ten minutes, or it could have been for an hour. We were just determined to put as much distance between the mob and us as possible. Eventually, we tumbled down an embankment, muddy water splashing up our legs, and hid there, waiting for the chasers to pass.

We held our breath, trying not to make a sound. Finally, after a few minutes had passed, Damian whispered, "I think they're gone."

I realized that we had no way of navigating back through the woods. We had been in such a blind panic we had failed to take note of a possible way out. So, instead, we took the opportunity to walk through the woods, catching our breath.

And then, we heard a crunching of twigs beneath a booted foot.

Damian rolled his eyes. "Oh, for fuck's sake!" he exclaimed, getting ready to bolt.

"Wait, wait!" the figure shouted, and we could see he was joined by another figure, a woman in her mid-twenties. It was the two acolytes who had made it possible for us to escape in the first place.

"How did you find us?" asked Damian.

"We led the mob on a bit of a goose chase," said the woman. "And besides, parents always find their way back home to their children."

40

Even after all the night's revelations, I still couldn't bring myself to believe that my parents were standing here in front of me. "You're not my mom and dad."

"We are," insisted the male acolyte.

"Prove it," I said. "Tell us something only we would know."

It was the female acolyte that spoke next. "When I first took you and Damian to that burger bar, you had lettuce and tomato on your burger. You asked me to pick out all of the vegetables for you even though I told you several times-"

"-it would be good for me in the long run," I finished disbelievingly.

We couldn't believe it. Our parents, through some bizarre twist of fate, had been returned to us, albeit in the form of Deacon's acolytes.

Damian and I fell to the ground simultaneously, and suddenly, we weren't grown men fleeing through the woods from psychotic worshippers. Instead, we were two kids stranded at a campsite, wondering why mommy and daddy had left us.

Mom and Dad moved forwards, hugging us close to their robed chests. "I'm so sorry we left you," said Dad. "There are so many things I want to tell you."

Drying his eyes, Damian said, "Well, best start, then."

"You really want to do this now?" asked Mom.

"We can walk and talk," insisted Damian. "We've spent too many years not knowing the truth to just walk away."

"All right," said Dad. "But we need to get going. They will be on the move."

As we walked through the woods, the most bizarre family outing anyone could have possibly imagined, Dad spoke. "I suppose I'll start at the beginning."

"I used to be a bit of a drifter. I left my hometown with very few qualifications, and I spent my time moving from place to place, trying to find anywhere that would take me on for work. Your mother was working as a waitress in one of the towns I stopped in."

"We started chatting," interjected Mom. "And it was very much love at first sight."

"One night, she was leaving the diner after a late shift. It was very dark and not the kind of neighborhood where a young woman should walk home alone," said Dad, and I remembered the dating tips he had given me as a kid. 'Always make your partner feel safe with you.' I could see now where that mindset had come from.

"Anyway, we were walking home when we saw a homeless man that Nancy usually passed on her route to and from her shift. Nancy had always taken the time to make sure that he had a bit of loose change, often bringing him leftovers from the diner. She was worried about him, wanted to make sure he was all right. I would have just gladly walked on and left him, but your mother was a far more empathetic person than me." He paused, and cleared his throat. "That night, Nancy approached him and started to speak, at which point, he started convulsing."

Mom spoke up. "And then there was this blue mist coming out of him. I'll never forget that."

I thought back to the incident with Arnold.

"Next thing we know, there was this ghost standing over us, looking at the corpse of the homeless man. Before we could do anything, we were attacked by figures in robes and abducted," said Mom, shuddering. "I thought it was some sort of secret police. Later, we would discover that they were acolytes, members of the Sainthood Church."

"In hindsight, the police would have been better," said Dad.

"So, they took us to this church, and there we met Minister Deacon."

"And she was the same age then as she is now?" asked Damian.

"Very much so," said Mom. "We thought that she was going to kill us both. But instead, she told us that we were blessed to witness a divine miracle. She could see the energy from our... aura, I think she called it. Energy that was like fuel to her. She said if we wanted to know more about the other side, we were invited to join the Sainthood Church. At the time, Derrick was drifting with no real place of his own, and I was on thin ice with my parents who were telling me it was about time I found a husband."

"So, you joined the church," I said disapprovingly.

"We thought it was just a way to keep a roof over our heads," said Dad defensively. "We had no idea what we were letting ourselves in for. And we both thought that it was a chance to be part of something bigger than ourselves. I'm not proud of the decisions we made back then. I wish we had told them where they could take their offer. And over time, your mother and I grew close to one another."

"So, you joined a cult and helped them transplant souls?" I asked. I had spent so many years with the perfect image of my parents to sustain me, but now that image was shattered.

"We thought we were giving people a divine exposure to the supernatural," protested Mom weakly.

"That was what you believed or what Deacon believed?" asked Damian. "Either way, you still went along with it."

"We were young and stupid," said Dad. "You're telling me you've never made a poor choice you wish you could take back?"

Sensing that Damian's attitude wasn't helping, I tried to pursue a less sensitive line of questioning. "So, what made you walk away from the church? I'm assuming that's what happened?"

"I became pregnant with Damian," said Mom. "It was both the best moment of my life and the scariest. The pregnancy made us look at the whole world differently. It was a literal 'I was blind, but now I can see' moment. We realized that the world we inhabited was not one a child should be exposed to."

"So, we stole some money from the church," said Dad. "And we left in the middle of the night. We both got real jobs and used the money to put ourselves in a motel until we could get a place of our own. You might remember that place, Damian."

Looking at Damian's face, I could see he did remember. "I remember that room from when I was little."

"We tried to make a decent life for ourselves," explained Dad. "We knew that Deacon would not let a slight go unpunished, but we also knew we couldn't go to the police and tell them what we knew. Best case scenario, they'd laugh us out of the station, thinking we were crazy."

I couldn't disagree with them on that point.

"Worst case scenario, we would have been arrested and charged with accessory to murder," added Mom.

"So you were happy to take the gamble," said Damian.

"They would have taken you away from us," said Mom. "You two were our second chance at a good life. We didn't want to mess with that."

Dad sighed. "We had thought that if enough time passed, maybe Deacon would forget about us both. But that's the trouble with freezing someone in time. The grudges never die either. And she sent people after us. She couldn't have done it herself."

"Why?" I asked.

"Sainthood draws its power from the spirits around here. Because Deacon draws on the energy from the spirits, this power is the sole thing keeping her alive. And if she was to leave this border, let's say, go to the edge of the town, for example, she'd lose that protection. I'll let your imagination fill in the rest."

It did. And it wasn't a pretty sight.

"Unfortunately, Deacon had powerful friends in the supernatural world; spirits and other people warped by her philosophy. They finally caught up with us on a

camping trip. We knew that the game was up. And they…"
Dad went silent as he relived the moment of his death, still
frozen there now. Mom put a comforting hand on his
shoulder as he steadied himself.

Composing himself, he continued, "We were exposed
to the supernatural, hence generating an energy around us
that Deacon could draw on. We were practically tied on a
string. No matter where we ran, her followers would have
found us eventually. Frankly, I'm amazed that we
managed to outrun them for as long as we did."

"But I'm glad we did," Mom added quickly. "Because
we got to enjoy those wonderful years with you boys. We
treasured those more than anything."

"So we ran out into the woods," said Dad. "We knew
they would find us eventually. But you boys hadn't
witnessed any supernatural events, and thus, you would
both be safe."

41

All these years, I had wondered what had happened to my parents. Finally, to hear them confess both the best and worst sides of themselves was too much to bear.

And I certainly seemed to be doing a better job of hiding my feelings than Damian, who gave a short, exasperated laugh.

"I can't believe this!" he exclaimed. "So many years I've spent thinking on the 'maybes' and the 'could have beens', trying to imagine what would have happened if we had done things differently. And now, I hear that Liam and I didn't have any choice in the matter. We were screwed the moment we came out of the womb!"

"That's not true, Damian!" protested Mom. "We did it to protect you!"

"'Protect us?'" repeated Damian. "We've spent most of our lives in a constant train wreck, careening from one disaster to another. Liam experiencing meltdown after meltdown, and me sabotaging anything good that came my way. I used to hate you guys for leaving us! For not being there to do the things a parent should do for their kids!" I could see he was no longer trying to hold back the tears.

Mom moved towards him. "Damian, we're not proud of our past. Not just for the things we did for Deacon, but because both of your lives could have been so different were it not for the decisions that your parents made."

"We spent years trying to find out what happened to you!" said Damian. "Why couldn't you tell us, just give us a sign that you were there, watching over us?"

"It doesn't work like that, son," said Dad. "We might have some presence, but we can't actually communicate with you. We have no powers of our own."

"Then how are you able to take over the bodies of two of Deacon's cronies?" I asked, letting emotion give way to curiosity.

"Because the more spiritual people are gathered together, the more power they hold. They can take over bodies at will. But unless they have been stabbed with the ceremonial dagger, the change won't be permanent. If anything, the spirit will burn up the body after a few hours. So, if we stay in these bodies for any longer than a few hours, the hosts will die."

"Given who they're helping, I can't bring myself to cry a river," said Damian.

"We never had the strength to overpower Deacon before you two came along. We know all about the experience you two have had," said Dad warmly. "It fills me with pride to know that you have been able to help people, that you have given them a sense of peace, even undo some of the damage that Deacon has done."

187

"I can't hear any more of this!" shouted Damian, and then he took off through the woods.

"Damian!" I called after him. "Damian, for God's sake, we've got to think rationally about this!"

"Liam, our whole life has been a lie! Every shitty thing that has come our way is because mom and dad bought into that demented cult!" He yelled back. "I preferred it when I thought our parents were dead!"

I let him go and turned back to my parents.

"I didn't want it to be like this," said Mom through broken sobs as Dad held her in his arms.

I wanted to tell her it was all right, that everything would be all right. I wanted to convey some sense that we understood.

But at the same time, I didn't want to comfort her. I didn't want to tell her that it was all right. Because the damage had already been done. Their poor judgment had ricocheted to create decades of trauma.

But there was still a way we could make things right.

"Do you think we can kill Deacon?" I asked.

Mom and Dad looked at each other before Mom said, "It's not possible. As long as she's wearing that ring, and she's living off the energy residue from spirits, she is untouchable."

"Well then, we'll have to render her touchable," I said.

"It was hard enough getting out of there!" exclaimed Dad. "And now you're saying you want to go back in?"

"Our lives aren't the only ones that Deacon has destroyed. How many people have suffered over the years – decades, even – because of her? I've seen that woman up close. She's got a taste for power, and she won't settle for anything less. She won't stop, and we're in a position to do something." With a heavy heart, I continued, "We can't change what happened to us. But we can at least make sure no one else has to endure the same pain we have."

Mom and Dad looked at each other, the decision nearly finalized, but I could see that there was something that they weren't saying aloud. "What?" I asked.

"That ring is the only thing linking us to this world," said Dad. "The ring gets destroyed-"

"-and we pass on," finished Mom.

I couldn't take it, the unfairness of it all. We had gone from trying to uncover the truth about our parents, to reuniting with them again, to learning the ugly facts, and now I would have to say goodbye to them all over again.

"There's so much I wanted to say to you both," I gasped out. "It's not fair."

"I know it isn't fair," said Mom. "If we're going to stop Deacon, that's the way it needs to be." She took my head in her hands and looked directly into my eyes. "But know this, love. I am so proud of the men you have become. I'm glad that we were able to see you again."

I held up a hand, not wanting to burst into tears. "Hold off on the declarations. Damian should be around for this."

And so, we started to make our way out of the woods, conscious of the danger lying ahead of us.

42

There had been so much running in our lives. So much looking back, never looking forward. But as we strode through the woods into a clearing, I felt a renewed sense of purpose. We were going to put a stop to Deacon once and for all. I didn't know how, but we would accomplish this mission.

I wished that Damian was here so I could adequately brief him on what needed to happen. I hoped he could find it in himself to forgive our parents, at least for the next few hours, because there was a chance we would never get an opportunity like this again.

We could see the lights from the town just visible through the trees, and as we walked into the clearing, there she was.

Deacon stood opposite us, blocking our entrance into Deliverance. "Nancy. Derrick," she said courteously.

"Deacon," said Dad.

"So, the prodigal ones returned," said Deacon. "Taking over two of my acolytes, I see."

"It's better than the fate you had lined up for them," said Mom.

"I granted them divineness. If you truly believed that I subjected them to a fate worse than death, you wouldn't have abetted me for as long as you did."

Mom didn't reply. There was nothing she could say that would repel Deacon's accurate accusations.

So I spoke up instead. "And if you really bought into that divineness shit, you'd happily have your body up for grabs."

Now it was Deacon's turn to be silently furious, but she recovered quickly and said, "We are not born equal. Some are born with greater powers than others. Jesus was anointed to lead the early flock. As I shall lead the current generation."

"Well, you won't be leading them very far," I said. "Not unless you want to put all those years back on the clock."

Deacon looked over at my mom and dad. "I see tongues have been wagging." She twirled the ring on her finger as though ensuring it was still there before continuing. "You know, Nancy, I took you and your partner for soft-peddling sycophants. You're both truly more capable than I gave either of you credit for. It's a shame you never showed any initiative when you had the chance to take me off the board altogether."

"Oh, I know," said Mom. "The biggest regret of my life was that I didn't kill you when I had the chance. But... better late than never."

"Oh, I don't think so," said Deacon. "By my reckoning, you are burning up those bodies quite quickly. I'd say they've only got a few more hours left."

"Enough time for us to kill you," said Dad.

"Not if I get there first."

"I don't know if your eyesight is failing, but there's three of us and one of you," I said, hoping that my fear didn't shine through in my voice.

"Do you seriously think I'd come here alone?"

She whistled, and a legion appeared behind her. It was a squadron of both living and dead, the spirits of people who had died generations ago. The living stepped forward, and the dead entered their bodies, a mass emergence taking place.

"Still fancy your chances?" asked Deacon smugly. "All of these men and women will happily lay their lives down before mine. In fact, most of them probably already have at some point."

She stepped forward, knowing that I had no weapons to fend her off.

"I have never been one for getting my hands dirty," she said. "But your death should be a symbolic one. As a child, I have always loved the stories from the bible. And you know the one that resonated with me the most? That of Cain and Abel. I've always wanted to see that particular story play out in real life. And now, I think I'll get my wish."

And then one of her minions stepped forward.

I gasped. It was Damian.

He stood tall, looking directly at me, and I could see in his eyes a burning desire to kill.

"Damian?" I asked.

"Damian's taken a leave of absence," he responded.

"Leave him out of this," cried Mom.

"Oh, but you see, Nancy, your son has so much potential. The aura surrounding him is powerful. You see, most of my acolytes incinerate after a few hours, but the exposure that Damian has had to the supernatural, it's like having the world's biggest battery." She pointed to me. "And you're next."

"Over my dead body."

"Oh, that can be arranged," cackled Deacon. With a click of her fingers, Damian moved forward, and I could see that he was brandishing a crowbar. I took a step back, not wanting to hurt my brother.

"Let's leave the boys to it," said Deacon. "As for the deserters," she faced her army and pointed to my parents. "They are all yours."

At her signal, the acolytes charged forward, brandishing weapons, ready to kill.

To their credit, Mom and Dad stood their ground, facing them head-on, while I faced down my brother.

"Damian, if you're in there," I said, just in time to dodge a swing of the crowbar. "You don't have to do this! You don't want to do this!"

"Want has nothing to do with it," said Damian drowsily, as though he was waking up from a slumber. "You know the ironic thing? We thought we'd have to chase you to the ends of the Earth. But you came to us. I'm not sure whether that decision was brave or stupid."

I tried to tell myself that this creature wasn't my brother talking, that it was just some undead monster speaking from beyond the grave through Damian's lips.

"It's me! Your brother, Liam!"

Damian swung the crowbar, unphased, and this time the blow connected. I screamed in pain and fell to the ground, clutching my knee.

"You know," said the imposter. "You and your brother act as though you were each other's crutch over the years, keeping each other sane. But in truth, you were only holding each other back. You could have achieved greatness separately, but you clung to each other like a life raft. The only thing you achieved together was to fall into this trap."

"You can't kill me," I said. "You heard Deacon; you need me alive."

"Aye, that we do," said the imposter. "But we don't need you in the best of shape. I'm merely going to inflict enough damage to leave you at the brink of death. And then, I'll depart your brother's body so that he can enjoy his handiwork."

I continued to fight, trying to block both the imposter's words and the swinging crowbar. I struggled to my feet, my knee exploding in a firewall of pain.

The imposter stepped back, bemused by my effort. "I don't know why you bother," he said. "You honestly think you have a chance against us? Do you think you will turn the tide in a decades-long war? You lost before you were even born into this world. It doesn't matter how long it takes, a decade, a century. This Eden is ours. And Deacon will show us the way. And you will be marching into the new world alongside us, whether you want to or not. And don't worry, we will make sure you live long enough to see us claim a few souls."

"That's never going to happen," I said determinedly. "Because Damian won't let it, will you, Damian?"

"He can't hear you," said the imposter.

"You've just gone on about how strong my brother is?" I said. "Well, he's not going to let anything happen to me."

I began to recite a story, blocking the crowbar once again and fighting back with a weapon of my own.

"I remember when we were kids, shortly after we lost mom and dad. Kids at school could be cruel. They were always picking on me, particularly. I remember they held me down and emptied a trash bin over my head one time. You saw what they were doing, and you came over to stop them."

I had to briefly pause the story to avoid another blow. I didn't know how much longer I could keep this up.

"It was four of them against you. You could have just walked away. You knew you would get a beating, but you kept on those bullies. You fought them all for me. At that moment, I knew you would always be there for me. I knew you would never let me down. And you never have."

The final words left my mouth in a strangled cry as the crowbar connected with my shoulder, and I fell to the ground, landing in a patch of wet leaves.

The imposter knelt and placed Damian's hands on either side of my head, gripping tightly. It felt like an eternity was passing as I waited for the final killing blow.

But it didn't come. Instead, Damian spluttered and coughed. The air around him turned blue, and he screamed in agony as the imposter flew from his body.

Damian leaned in close and whispered in my ear, "Thanks for not giving up on me." Then, he released his grip on me, and my body crumpled back down to the earth.

Damian picked up the crowbar, raised it above his head, and had just enough time to get one word out.

"Scream."

And then he brought the crowbar crashing down.

43

When I came to, the first sensation that hit me was the feeling of cold dirt pouring into the shallow grave. After that, an avalanche of pain.

Every part of me ached. My brain sent a signal down to my limbs as if to confirm that they still worked, but I could not will them into action.

In some ways, the pain greeted me like an old friend. Not the physical pain, but the emotional kind that exploded tenfold in the past twenty-four hours, turning my entire world into hell on Earth.

I opened my eyes and saw the glistening full moon partially visible behind the mass of trees. I wondered if werewolves were roaming about the forest. An absurd thought, but after everything I had uncovered, I wouldn't be surprised.

There was a strange, haunting beauty to the world around me. It was as though now that there was nothing left to torment me, I could finally appreciate the world in what little time I had left.

I tried to speak, to plead for help, but what passed through my lips was a series of rough, scratchy noises, as though my throat had been scraped raw.

Another layer of dirt fell on top of me. Some of it landed in my mouth.

I made the decision not to die here and now. I pulled myself up, the dirt falling away as I rose, looking my would-be killer in the face...only to see my brother Damian staring back at me.

"Thank God you do a good job of playing dead, or we'd both be screwed," he said, reaching down and offering me a hand.

I took it gratefully as Damian pulled me into a hug. "I can't not have you in my life bro, even if you are a pain in the ass."

"Runs in the family," I acknowledged. "So, what do we do now?"

I ran through the events again in my head. When Damian had brought the crowbar crashing down earlier, it had landed on the ground beside me, but no one was the wiser; everyone was preoccupied with the larger fight taking place.

Deacon had seen what appeared to be an unconscious body.

"A shame," she had said as Mom's scream rang through the air. "We could have made use of him."

"Well," said Damian, imitating the imposter. "At least we know he won't be causing us any more trouble in the future."

"True," said Deacon. "Dispose of the body."

"As you wish, Minister."

As she turned her attention back to the battle, I had continued to play dead as Damian dragged my body out of the way and dumped me into a shallow grave.

He must have disappeared for some time because I remember lying there for some time, trying to decide whether to take the risk and get up or stay put.

After I had gotten to my feet, Damian pulling me out of the shallow grave, the dirt falling from me as though I had risen from the dead – which, technically, I had done – Damian showed me a bag. "Borrowed this from the Sainthood Church."

Inside were several ancient relics, weapons, everything that Deacon had used to wage her unholy war.

"We have a chance to stop this once and for all, bro," said Damian.

"Damian, I learned something," I start. "If we get that ring off Deacon's finger and destroy it, she loses her protection from all the other spirits. But then, if it is destroyed, Mom and Dad pass on."

Damian stopped. I could tell he had a million things he had wanted to say and a few that he wanted to take back. Once again, he would not have the time for either.

"It's not fair," he said, remembering when he had been forced into the role of my caretaker far too young. "Isn't there anything we can do? Preserve the ring or something?"

I wanted more than anything to tell him that that was possible. I really did. If I could have seen any possible avenue of having a bit more time with Mom or Dad, I would have taken it. But we were weighing up two undead lives against the rest of the world.

In the end, it wasn't even a choice.

"It's what they would want," I said with a heavy heart.

Nodding his head in agreement, Damian sniffed and wiped his eyes. "I just wish we had more time."

"So do I, Damian. So do I."

Damian grabbed the bag, and we made our way back to the clearing. We crouched under cover of foliage, observing the scene before us.

Mom and Dad had managed to get a few good hits in, but they were fighting in bodies clearly feeling the spiritual strain of containing their souls. They had been overwhelmed so quickly; it hadn't been a fair match from the start.

But Deacon hadn't opted to kill them outright. We watched as they knelt on the ground, their hands on their heads, their bodies struggling to contain their spirits for much longer.

"Last time I killed you," said Deacon. "I wasn't there to see it in person. So, I didn't care how they killed you or how long it took. So, now that I have been gifted a second chance, I'm going to take my time with you."

"Allow me!" Damian called out as he made his way into the clearing, signaling for me to stay put. He hid the ceremonial dagger behind his back as he approached Deacon, wielding the crowbar in an outstretched hand. "I think there's something poetic about a son killing his own parents."

Deacon smiled. He was pandering to her sense of sadism, and it was working like a charm. "Brilliant idea," she said. "You may do the honors."

"I have been waiting for this for a long time," said Damian, concealing the dagger and preparing to bring the crowbar down on his father, only to turn at the last second and stab Deacon in the chest.

Deacon stepped back, stunned by the action, her hands groping for her chest in shock, and in the commotion, Damian plucked the ring off her finger.

"Wait! Noooo!" screamed Deacon through bloodied lips.

"I'm done waiting," said Damian as he brought the crowbar down on the ring, shattering the jewel that lay inside.

"No…" shrieked Deacon, scrambling over to the shattered emerald. But it was too late. Nothing could undo what had already been set in motion.

The spirits occupying the bodies of the acolytes drifted out of them as though being sucked out. The empty bodies dropped to the ground, lifeless. The spirits rose in the air, hovering like fireflies before they all converged on Deacon.

They flew directly into her, nesting themselves in her body. Deacon could feel the full weight of a hundred souls eating away at her. She tried to scream, but no sound emerged from her lips.

And then, before our eyes, she began to crumble. It started with her hands before quickly spreading up through Deacon's arms to her body, and then her face as she turned to dust and disintegrated. Finally, only a pile of dust remained.

"Earth to Earth. Ashes to ashes. Dust to dust," declared Damian.

I stumbled out of the clearing, limping, my knee still battered from the crowbar.

"Is she dead?" I asked.

"Looks like it," said Damian, stamping on the pile of dust that had once been Deacon.

We were interrupted by a faint glow and turned to see our parents standing before us, their spirits taking on their actual human forms. The same faces they had worn the day they had died.

"You did it," said Mom.

"We couldn't be prouder of you," said Dad.

As if suddenly compelled to take back everything he had said earlier, Damian rushed forward to hug them, only for the hug to pass right through.

"Why can't we have more time?" pleaded Damian.

"You'll have all the time you need now, boys," said Mom.

"Go out there and lead a good life, raise a family of your own," instructed Dad. "Leave all of this behind."

They began to fade away, and there was no way to stop the tears. We both wept as our parents departed for the last time, blowing a kiss before they were gone forever.

And my brother and I were left alone once again.

EPILOGUE

I surveyed the two freshly planted gravestones in the cemetery, a winter coat protecting me from the autumn chill. I leaned on a crutch; my knee was still sore from Damian's assault. The winter weather brought with it fresh feelings of pain.

Damian walked up to join me. "Feels odd, finally having a grave to visit."

"I know," I said. "But we did it, Damian. We avenged mom and dad, and we probably saved a lot more people along the way."

"You know there's always going to be someone like Deacon, right?" said Damian. "Someone's always going to be looking for dangerous, supernatural power."

"Oh, yeah, definitely," I agreed. "But as far as I'm concerned, our part in the story is done. We may not have the answers we wanted, but we certainly got the ones we needed."

"I have to tell you, Meredith called me yesterday," began Damian hesitantly. He had been seeing a lot of Meredith over the last month. I was happy for him. She was a sweet woman, and she was probably one of the only people who could help him make sense of all of this. "She mentioned an incident at the local hospital. Something about a child patient who shows all the signs of possession. Can't hurt to look into it."

"Maybe," I said. I couldn't deny the pull the supernatural had over me. Even though I had promised my parents I would try and live an ordinary life; maybe I could never outrun the supernatural. Perhaps the ghosts of the past would always be with me, forever haunting my every move.

I tried not to think about what the future held for us. I just wanted to focus on the here and now. I had my brother, my best friend, the one constant in my life. I knew that whatever life would throw my way, it would be a lot easier to tackle with Damian by my side.

Damian sighed deeply. Then he smiled and said, "Damn, it feels so good to be alive right now."

He was right, of course. It was an excellent time to be alive.

We left the graveyard together, leaving the ghosts in the past, ready to re-join the world of the living.

The End.

Thank you for reading *The Hidden Graveyard: The Whisper Investigations Trilogy.* It means a lot to me that you bought my book and I hope you enjoyed reading it!

If you liked this book, I would really appreciate an honest review on Amazon. I love to read what you have to say.

Scan the QR Code with your smartphone and leave me your feedback!

GET EXCLUSIVE FREE NOVELLA

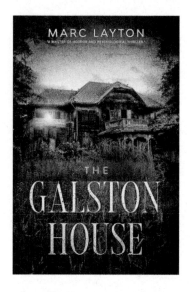

Don't forget to subscribe to my newsletter and join my VIP Readers Club for information on upcoming releases, plus you receive a free copy of The Galston House!

This exclusive novella is for new members of the VIP Readers Club.

Are you ready? Take out your camera app, make sure it can clearly see the code, and wait for the notification to appear. That's it!

ALSO BY MARC LAYTON

THE LAKE HAS EYES
THE HAUNTING OF BRIDGE MANOR TRILOGY

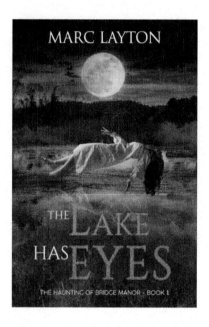

A mysterious house, a lake shrouded in secrets, and a malicious spirit on the hunt...

When Rachel arrives at the dilapidated Bridge Manor, she knew something was wrong. The run-down house and its eerie, ominous-looking lake gave her the creeps – no matter how much her parents tried to convince her it only needed repairs and a fresh coat of paint.

As Rachel struggles to recover after her coma and rekindle her bond with her family, she begins to befriend their distrustful neighbors... and she discovers the harrowing story behind the manor and its lake. A ghost haunts these cold waters – one that wants her dead.

Entangled in a web of malicious spirits and horrifying happenings, Rachel must use all of her wits and bravery to rescue herself, her brother, and her parents before they fall prey to the spirits haunting the lake.

Can Rachel manage to convince her family that the stories behind Bridge Manor are true? Or will the Lady of the Lake claim her next victims?

Artfully blending a ghost story with a dash of horror and suspense, *The Lake Has Eyes* is a chilling and memorable tale that is perfect for fans of all things paranormal.

Start reading! Take out your camera app, make sure it can clearly see the code, and wait for the notification to appear. That's it!

THE TASTER
INVESTIGATING HORROR SERIES

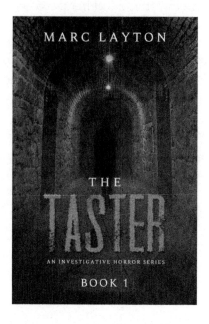

A labyrinthian cellar. A priceless wine collection. And a vengeful spirit who guards it for eternity.

Hidden in the darkest depths of the famous wine taster Matthew Boudin's cellar lies a secret – a collection of some of the rarest and most expensive wines the world has ever seen. Guarded by a maze of pitch-black corridors – and the embalmed corpse of the late Boudin himself – the collection has stood untouched for years.

Professor Aldous Crane doesn't believe in ghosts. Despite writing about the occult for over thirty years, he views their stories as a bit of fun and nothing more. But when he's called to investigate Boudin's infamous cellar, he soon realizes that the truth is something far more sinister.

If you love thrilling supernatural and occult stories packed with hair-raising suspense and tension which will keep you on the edge of your seat, then you won't want to miss *The Taster.*

Start reading! Take out your camera app, make sure it can clearly see the code, and wait for the notification to appear. That's it!

SLEEPLESS

THE EVERGREEN MOTEL SERIES

Best Horror Book of the Month April 2020 Award - manybooks.net

Kyle's threatening message hang in the air as Aly hits the country road, desperate to find safety. Her violent ex-boyfriend persists to hunt her down. The farther she escapes from Kyle, the more threatening his messages become.

He will stop at nothing to get her back.

Aly constantly reaches for the gun in her pocket — the only thing that is keeping her sane. After two hours of non-stop driving, the tension of the day starts to weigh heavy on her. She turns into the parking lot of The Evergreen Motel, a sleepy reprieve nestled in the woods.

However, what she thought was the perfect refuge slowly turns into something more sinister. The moment Aly lays down to sleep, strange things begin to occur. Paranoia, nightmares, and loud screams cut through the air.

Start reading! Take out your camera app, make sure it can clearly see the code, and wait for the notification to appear. That's it!

ABOUT THE AUTHOR

Marc Layton is the internationally bestselling horror author of The Haunting Of Bridge Manor, The Evergreen Motel and The Evil Inside. The only child of American expats, he grew up on a farm in northern Germany, went to boarding school in a remote part of Scandinavia and then returned to his familial roots for University in New Hampshire where he then settled. As an avid traveler, a voracious reader and a professional antiques dealer, Layton is never at a loss for inspiration and ever since he can remember he's been consumed by the things that go bump in the night. Layton lives and works out of a cottage near the water in Portsmouth, NH and spends his free time hiking with his wife and trusty Australian Shepard Lily.

Visit https://linktr.ee/MarcLayton to learn more or find Marc Layton on social @authormarclayton

Take out your camera app, make sure it can clearly see the code, and wait for the notification to appear. That's it!

Printed in Great Britain
by Amazon

83223327R00129